Dear Reader,

Isn't it amazing how swiftly the years have flown past? I marvel at all the changes, yet one thing has never changed: the satisfaction to be found in reading a good romance. Twenty years ago our romances were somewhat different. They mirrored the times, as popular fiction usually does. In many ways they were more naïve, as were we. It seems in retrospect as though the edges were softer, but then, maybe that's only in my imagination.

I've written a Cinderella story. The old fairy tales, the legends and myths still persist, don't they? Is there anyone among us who doesn't long for a happy ending?

Here you have it. Always, in a traditional romance. It's a given. And I give this one to you with my blessings and my hopes for all our happy endings.

My thanks to you, the readers, to the wonderful people at Silhouette, to the many friends I've made both there and among my fans—and the many more I hope to make in the future.

Sincerely,

Dear Reader,

From the enchantment of first loves to the wonder of second chances, Silhouette Romance demonstrates the power of genuine emotion. This month we continue our yearlong twentieth anniversary celebration with another stellar lineup, including the return of beloved author Dixie Browning with *Cinderella's Midnight Kiss*.

Next, Raye Morgan delivers a charming marriage-of-convenience story about a secretary who is *Promoted—To Wife!* And Silhouette Romance begins a new theme-based promotion, AN OLDER MAN, which highlights stories featuring sophisticated older men who meet their matches in younger, inexperienced women. Our premiere title is *Professor and the Nanny* by reader favorite Phyllis Halldorson.

Bestselling author Judy Christenberry unveils her new miniseries, THE CIRCLE K SISTERS, in *Never Let You Go*. When a millionaire businessman wins an executive assistant at an auction, he discovers that he wants her to be *Contractually His...*forever. Don't miss this conclusion of Myrna Mackenzie's THE WEDDING AUCTION series. And in Karen Rose Smith's *Just the Husband She Chose,* a powerful attorney is reunited in a marriage meant to satisfy a will.

In coming months, look for new miniseries by some of your favorite authors. It's an exciting year for Silhouette Books, and we invite you to join the celebration!

Happy reading!

Mary-Theresa Hussey

Mary-Theresa Hussey
Senior Editor

Please address questions and book requests to:
Silhouette Reader Service
U.S.: 3010 Walden Ave., P.O. Box 1325, Buffalo, NY 14269
Canadian: P.O. Box 609, Fort Erie, Ont. L2A 5X3

CINDERELLA'S MIDNIGHT KISS

Dixie Browning

ROMANCE™

Published by Silhouette Books

America's Publisher of Contemporary Romance

This book is dedicated to Silhouette
and twenty wonderful, memorable years.
And to two tough guys who did their best
to keep me from finishing it.
Hurricanes Dennis and Floyd!

 SILHOUETTE BOOKS

ISBN 0-373-19450-1

CINDERELLA'S MIDNIGHT KISS

Copyright © 2000 by Dixie Browning

Visit Silhouette at www.eHarlequin.com

Printed in U.S.A.

Books by Dixie Browning

DIXIE BROWNING

celebrated her sixty-fifth book for Silhouette with the publication of *Texas Millionaire* in 1999. She has also written a number of historical romances with her sister under the name Bronwyn Williams. A charter member of Romance Writers of America, and a member of Novelists, Inc., Dixie has won numerous awards for her work. She lives on the Outer Banks of North Carolina.

IT'S OUR 20th ANNIVERSARY!
We'll be celebrating all year,
Continuing with these fabulous titles,
On sale in June 2000.

Romance

#1450 Cinderella's Midnight Kiss
Dixie Browning

#1451 Promoted–To Wife!
Raye Morgan

 AN OLDER MAN
#1452 Professor and the Nanny
Phyllis Halldorson

The Circle K Sisters
#1453 Never Let You Go
Judy Christenberry

The WEDDING AUCTION
#1454 Contractually His
Myrna Mackenzie

#1455 Just the Husband She Chose
Karen Rose Smith

Desire

MAN of the MONTH
#1297 Tough To Tame
Jackie Merritt

#1298 The Rancher and the Nanny
Caroline Cross

MATCHED IN MONTANA
#1299 The Cowboy Meets His Match
Meagan McKinney

#1300 Cheyenne Dad
Sheri WhiteFeather

 The Baby Bank
#1301 The Baby Gift
Susan Crosby

#1302 The Determined Groom
Kate Little

Intimate Moments

 The WILDES of WYOMING
#1009 The Wildes of Wyoming–Ace
Ruth Langan

#1010 The Best Man
Linda Turner

#1011 Beautiful Stranger
Ruth Wind

#1012 Her Secret Guardian
Sally Tyler Hayes

#1013 Undercover with the Enemy
Christine Michels

#1014 The Lawman's Last Stand
Vickie Taylor

Special Edition

#1327 The Baby Quilt
Christine Flynn

#1328 Irish Rebel
Nora Roberts

#1329 To a MacAllister Born
Joan Elliott Pickart

 A Family Bond
#1330 A Man Apart
Ginna Gray

 DESERT ROGUES
#1331 The Sheik's Secret Bride
Susan Mallery

#1332 The Price of Honor
Janis Reams Hudson

Prologue

"This is my first diary, and I don't know exactly where to start. Mama always kept one, but I never did. She told me to read hers after she was gone so I would understand, but her personal things were packed away and I couldn't get to them for a long time.

"My name is Cynthia Danbury. I am fourteen and a half years old."

Fourteen and a half. Ten years ago. How very young I was then, she mused now.

"I'm called Cindy, which probably should be spelled Sendy because people are always sending me on errands. In case anyone ever reads this, I want it on record that Daddy was an inventor. He died before he could invent anything important that people would pay money for, but that didn't mean he never amounted to anything. Mama worked real hard at the truck stop to earn money for Daddy's experiments. She was not a worthless shantytown tramp who ruined a perfectly decent boy, like Aunt Stephenson told Uncle Henry she was, which is one of the reasons I'm writing this. To set the record straight.''

Looking back, Cindy could remember as if it were yesterday the first time she'd met her aunt Stephenson, her father's sister. Cindy had been about seven years old. They had just moved to Mocksville. Her father had taken her to a large white house, with a wide porch and stained glass panels beside the front door, to meet her aunt Lorna.

They'd been standing in the front hall, only now it was called a foyer. Her father had introduced her to a large woman in a black silk dress and told Cindy that this was her ''Aunt Lorna.''

''You may call me Mrs. Stephenson,'' the woman had corrected coldly. Her father had been furious. Cindy remembered hiding behind him and clinging to his hand. Over the years they had reached a compromise, she and her father's sister. Cindy called her Aunt S.

Picking up the diary again, she skipped a few pages and continued to read. ''Mama never went with us when we visited. I didn't understand why until years later, when I read her diary a long time after the accident.

''The accident was when Daddy and I were taking Mama to work, and this tank truck blew a tire and ran us off the road. Daddy was killed instantly. My hip was damaged. A nurse said it was crushed, but if that had been the case I'd have had to have a new one, and I didn't. Just a patch job.

"Anyway, Mama and I were both in the hospital and couldn't even go to Daddy's funeral. Aunt S. saw to everything, and I guess I'm grateful, but I resent it, too. I don't like to think about those days, so mostly I don't."

Cindy's hip never had healed properly. She still limped when she was tired, but the scar was barely visible. She'd been about eleven then. It had happened in November. She could remember starting her period the next May and thinking it had something to do with her hip, until her mother explained.

"Mama was surprised I didn't already know, and I guess I sort of did. They teach all about it in school, only it's different when it actually happens to you. Besides, whenever I have to listen to embarrassing stuff, I design hats in my mind. Big, fancy hats. The romantic kind with lots of nice floppy flowers."

Yes, and she still did, only now she did more than merely design them in her mind. Skimming a few more pages, Cindy marveled at how naive she'd been ten years earlier.

"Who I Am. In case I have children of my own one day and they need to know about their lina— lineage, I can't really help with it very much. I do know Mama's folks, the Scarboroughs, came from out near the coast somewhere, and there aren't any left closer than third cousin, once removed. But maybe this will be a starting place.

"Mama was real sad after Daddy died, and when she didn't get over it, it turned out that she had leukemia. I stayed with a neighbor while she was in the hospital, and when I'd visit her she tried to pretend everything was going to be all right, but we both knew better.

"Those were really bad times. I remember we played double sol and watched silly cartoons on TV. Sometimes we just sat and held hands. Once we laughed together over what she called my tacky taste, and she said I must have inherited it from her because we both liked big, gaudy hats with tons of fake flowers."

Cindy reached for the framed photograph on her bedside table, an out-of-focus snapshot of a very young woman wearing bell-bottom pants, a halter, a floppy-brimmed hat trimmed with sunflowers, and a broad, happy smile. Mama at age nineteen, holding her precious old Gibson guitar.

"I'm not going to talk about all that because it still hurts too much, but if anyone ever reads this, I want you to know that Aurelia Scarborough Danbury was the sweetest, bravest woman in the world. That's all I'm going to say about that.

"Anyway, after Mama died I went to live with Aunt Stephenson and Uncle Henry and my stepcousins, Maura and Stephanie, because in a town like ours, where everybody knows everybody's family all the way back to Year One, even when some of them live in big fancy houses like Aunt S. does and some live in trailer parks like we did, the whole town knows who's kin to who. (Or as Aunt S. would say, whom.) So when the social services lady said if the Stephensons wouldn't take me in they'd have to find me a foster home, poor Aunt S. didn't have much choice. I guess she could've explained, but people would still have talked, and Nice People don't get themselves talked about, according to Aunt S.

"Uncle Henry was more like family than Aunt S. Actually, neither of them was real family, but you know what I mean. He used to call me Radish on account of my hair, and give me a box of chocolates and a twenty-dollar bill every Christmas. I saved half the money for the Future and spent the rest on gifts, but the candy never lasted through the holidays. Steff and Maura both have a sweet tooth.

"I didn't really want to live there, but I didn't know what else to do, and anyway, when you're only twelve and a half, people don't listen to you. But I sort of liked Maura and Steff. Maura is two years older than I am, Steff three and a half years older. We've never had much in common. Since I'm smaller than either of them, I never have to worry about clothes, though. Maura always buys her jeans a size too small, and when Aunt S. catches her in them, she makes her give them to me. Same with T-shirts. Tight. Maura likes to show off her boobs, but I don't have any yet. I don't really like jeans very much, they're hot in the summertime and cold in the winter, but I guess they're pretty practical.

"Steff never wears jeans. She gives me dresses she doesn't want, usually the fancy kind that have to be dry-cleaned. Definitely not practical! Luckily, I'm good at mending and spot-cleaning, which they almost always need by the time I get them.

"You might have noticed I tend to ramble a lot. Mama used to say I had a brain like an overgrown flower garden. There's good stuff in it if you can ever find it under all the weeds.

"For the record, though, I'm truly grateful for Aunt S.'s kindness, which is why I can't just walk away and get on with my life, as much as I'm tempted to."

Oh, how many times she'd been tempted, but soon now…very soon, she would be ready.

"Well, Diary, here comes the hard part. It concerns something Aunt S. knew all along, but I didn't find out until years later when I finally got up the nerve to read Mama's diary. Which is one of the reasons I'm doing this—to set the record straight so my children and grandchildren, if any, will know what's what.

"I'm not a real Danbury. My biological father was a navy pilot who crashed on a training mission before I was even born. Mama said his name was Bill Jones and he was from somewhere in Virginia, which doesn't help much, but there it is, anyway.

"When Daddy married Mama, he gave me his name, which is probably why Aunt S. took me to live with her. Uncle Henry didn't mind. About Uncle Henry—he wears three-piece suits and walks to the office every morning and walks home every afternoon for a cigar, a drink and a nap. Maura looks a lot like him, but she's not as kind."

With a sigh, Cindy laid the diary aside and stared out the window at the house next door. Hitch was coming back. Which was why she'd dug out her old diary in the first place—because John Hale Hitchcock had figured in so many of her girlish fantasies back in her diary-keeping days.

When Mac had told her Hitch had agreed to be his best man, she'd nearly drowned in all those old daydreams. She would die of embarrassment if he ever found out, but he probably wouldn't even recognize her. She wasn't sure he'd really noticed her in those days, yet even after ten years she could remember him as if it had been only yesterday.

Of course, he'd have changed—he might even be married, although Mac hadn't mentioned a wife. But then, she herself had changed since the days when she'd thought he hung the moon. Not a whole lot, but at least she was no longer built like an ironing board.

Skimming over the middle part of the worn diary, Cindy picked up at her eighteenth birthday.

"Uncle Henry gave me my own car! I can't believe it! Now instead of bicycling all over town to do my Monday errands, I can drive. Maybe I should paint a sign on the side—something like Send Cindy, She's Fast, Reliable and Cheap.

"Aunt S. would have a hissy-fit."

Her uncle had died before her next birthday. She still missed him. "I think Aunt S. knows anyway," Cindy had written all those years ago. "The reason she doesn't say anything is because then she might have to give me an allowance to buy the stuff I absolutely have to have. I've done my best to earn my keep all these years by making myself useful, but I'll tell you this much, Diary. I might end up an old maid, but no way will I ever let Maura or Steff fix me up with another blind date. The one last month nearly tore my dress off. The one last week told dirty jokes and laughed when I blushed, and last night's date was so boring I nearly fell asleep while he was telling me about every job he ever held, from bag boy right on up to produce manager. I might not be rich or well-bred or pretty, but I deserve better than that.''

That was one thing that hadn't changed, Cindy told herself, laying the diary aside again. She deserved whatever she could make of her life. Once Steff's wedding was over, she was going to find a tiny apartment she could afford and turn her Monday job into a full-time thing until she saved enough to launch her dream career. One day, women would go back to wearing gorgeous, feminine, romantic hats, and when that happened, she would be ready.

If she still had enough energy left after this blasted wedding!

Chapter One

John Hale Hitchcock quietly hung up the phone and began to swear. He'd finally said yes, but that didn't mean he didn't have serious reservations. All his adult life he'd made it a policy to stay as far away from weddings as possible in case they were contagious. Especially weddings that required his active participation. What was it the shrinks called it? A defense mechanism?

Yeah, it was that and more.

He'd always had a feeling his own parents hated each other's guts, but were far too well bred to mention it. Add to that his mother's sporadic attempts to pair him up with one of her colleagues and it was no wonder he'd developed a jaded outlook on marriage.

He'd eventually learned to handle such things tactfully. In spite of his parents' dismay when he'd chosen engineering over law, Georgia Tech over

Yale, he wasn't a barbarian. At least he'd had the good manners not to come right out and admit to harboring a deep-seated aversion to pinstripes, brogans and button-down brains, a description that summed up those among his mother's younger female colleagues who considered her a role model. Now a highly esteemed federal judge, Janet Hale Hitchcock had never, not even in her junior-partner days, been a hands-on type mother.

Once she'd given up trying to hand over control of her only son to one of her right-minded colleagues, her matchmaking efforts had ceased. Now it was only his married friends who were forever trying to pair him up. Hitch put it down to the theory that misery liked company. His method of dealing with it was both tactful and efficient. Smile politely and run like hell. Having spent his formative years under the thumbs of domineering parents, in a home that had all the warmth of a refrigerator truck, he wasn't about to get caught in the marriage trap.

Mac's call had caught him at a weak moment. He'd just come back from a memorial service for another old classmate, dead of heart failure at the age of thirty-three, a year younger than Mac.

Life was risky business.

After pouring himself a drink, Hitch had been wallowing in a rare moment of philosophical nostalgia when Mac MacCollum had called to tell him about his upcoming wedding and ask him to act as best man.

"No thanks, my friend. In case you've forgotten, I'm severely allergic to weddings."

"Aw, come on, Hitch, you're my closest pal. I couldn't ask anyone else."

The two men had gone through four years at Georgia Tech together, Hitch on a football scholarship as his parents, both Yale law school graduates, had refused to condone such heresy. The day after graduation Mac and Hitch had joined the army together. Mac had then tried on half a dozen careers, while Hitch went to Harvard for his MBA. Through it all they'd never lost contact, due mostly to Mac's friendly persistence.

"You know, Mac," Hitch had remarked, "whining was never one of your more attractive traits."

"I'm not whining, man, I'm begging. Begging has more dignity than whining."

"Do I know the lucky lady?"

"You remember Steffie Stephenson? Lives next door to our house?"

Hitch would never forget the many weekends during their college years he'd spent in the rambling, friendly, comfortable old house in a small North Carolina town. The MacCollums' place, messy, noisy, filled with the aroma of Mama Mac's good cooking, was as different from the house he'd grown up in as night from day.

He also remembered the Stephenson sisters next door, Stephanie and...was it Mary? Marnie? Something like that.

And hadn't there been a third sister? He'd never actually met her, but he seemed to recall a red-haired kid scurrying around in the background.

"Yeah, I remember Steff," he said, sipping the one drink a day he allowed himself. "Word of advice, Mac. Get out before it's too late. Women need marriage. Men don't. Don't bother to question my logic—logic never was your strong suit—just take my word for it. Get out of Dodge.''

But Mac had talked him into it. Good old Mac, with his big ears, two left feet and ready grin. The guy could talk a dalmatian out of his spots. Hitch had hung up, having reluctantly agreed, and spent the next few minutes wondering how the devil Mac and Steff had ever got together. Unless she'd changed considerably since he'd last seen her, Stephanie Stephenson was a shallow little snob with a cover girl face and a one-cylinder brain.

Could she have finally wised up to the fact that Mac, for all he might act the clown, was a terrific guy? Or was it because, through a lot of hard work and some lucky breaks, he had parlayed the run-down ski resort he'd bought a few years ago into a thriving chain stretching all the way up into West Virginia?

Hitch polished off his drink, rose and stretched. He'd been working flat out for the past couple of years establishing his own business, JHH Designs, a small Richmond, Virginia, industrial design firm with a big future. He could use a break, and where better to take one than with the family who had treated him like one of their own?

That meant he'd be passing close to his parents' place on the drive from Richmond to Mocksville. Might as well make an effort to mend a few fences. It had been nearly a year since he'd seen them, and that last scene had not been pleasant.

Maybe, he thought with bitter amusement, he

could break the ice with a bit of gallows humor. *Hey folks, whaddya think, if Mac's marriage goes south the way most marriages seem to do these days, can the best man be nailed as an accessory after the fact?*

Oh, yeah, that would really crack 'em up.

Both his parents were lawyers with strong control tendencies. The trait had caused problems from the time Hitch was old enough to leave small, sticky fingerprints on every polished surface in the somber old house.

His mother, a small woman with iron-gray hair worn in a knot at the back of her head, could get more mileage from a lifted eyebrow than most people could from a loaded gun. His paternal grandfather had been a Supreme Court judge. Most of his cousins were lawyers or judges. Hitch had been slated to follow the family calling, only he'd had ideas of his own.

Major hassle. There was still a lot of residual bitterness, but one thing he'd inherited from both sides of the family was a streak of stubbornness a mile wide. He'd never actually won an argument with either of his folks, but at least he'd learned to minimize the damage by biting his tongue and walking out.

Matter of fact, the driving force behind his present success might easily be his determination to prove something to his parents.

Talk about childish.

"Two things I'll never be," Cindy muttered as she carted a stack of bone china to the kitchen to be washed, "are a caterer or a professional wedding planner."

She'd already broken the handle off one of the cups and had spent far too much valuable time on the phone to Greensboro to see if the china replacement center could match the pattern. Lucky for her it could.

Unlucky for her, it would cost her an arm and a leg, plus a drive to Greensboro at her own expense.

"Cindy, did you call the florist?"

"They're coming tomorrow to go over final plans."

"Cindy, is my dress back from the cleaner?"

"Be here in about an hour."

"Cindy, for goodness sake, I told you to air out my luggage! It smells like mildew!"

"It was cloudy when I got up, so I thought I'd better wait. If it doesn't clear up, I'll open all your cases and put them up in my room—that's always dry." And hot as Hades, as the attic wasn't air-conditioned.

The wedding was still days away, and already the guest rooms were filled with family here for the occasion, plus Steff's two attendants, both former college classmates. Cindy had run her legs right down to the nub trying to get all the rooms aired and made up, and all the china and crystal, which had to be hand washed and dried, ready for the rehearsal party, which had gone from a simple buffet to a combination ball and banquet.

Mac's folks were supposed to host the party but this was Aunt S.'s first wedding, and she was pulling out all the stops. What had started out to be a small, elegant home wedding was rapidly turning into a three-ring circus, in Cindy's estimation. A small thing like wedding protocol never stopped Aunt S.

All that in addition to trying to keep up with the ordinary demands of a demanding family, and Cindy was pooped. Just plain frazzled. And it was barely midafternoon, with three days to go until the wedding, after which there would be all the undoing and cleaning-up-after.

It was a good thing she was used to it, else she might have blown her redheaded stack.

"One of these days," she muttered, catching a glimpse of a cupcake wrapper under the hall table. One of these days she would have enough saved up to move out, and this would all seem like a crazy dream.

Meanwhile, it was a good thing she had the hide of an elephant and the backbone of a—well, whatever had the strongest backbone, which was what it took to survive when you had only yourself to depend on.

"Cynthia, have you been messing with my roses again?" Lorna Stephenson called out from the back parlor, where she was currently nursing a headache with a lavender-water-soaked cloth and a glass of medicinal brandy.

"No, ma'am, I haven't. I think Charlie was playing ball out there earlier, though. You might mention it to his mother."

If Cindy had had her way, she would have cut every flower in the yard and begged more from the neighbors, and done the wedding flowers herself. At least that way Aunt S.'s precious roses would be appreciated instead of trampled underfoot by a six-year-old hellion who didn't know the meaning of the word *no*.

But Aunt S. preferred the stiff, formal arrangements of the local florist over Cindy's big, cheerful armfuls of whatever happened to be blooming, all intertwined with wild honeysuckle and flowering blackberry vines.

Three days and counting. The house was gleaming. Cindy unexpectedly felt a surge of nostalgia—either that or the half sandwich she'd grabbed on the run for lunch hadn't settled properly.

Well, no, it was nostalgia, because while indigestion made her stomach burn, it didn't make her throat ache and her nose turn red. And after all, it was some sort of milestone, she supposed. The courtesy cousin she had practically grown up with was about to marry and leave home. Even though they'd never gotten along particularly well, she would miss her.

The wedding gown. Oh, yes, she reminded herself as she dashed up the back stairs—she really did need to offer a bit of advice, the thing was so blessed plain!

"Steff, about your gown," she said, rushing breathlessly into the big corner bedroom that had once been Aunt S. and Uncle Henry's. "It needs something, don't you think?"

"Don't you dare touch my wedding gown! It's a designer original!"

Steff described it as elegant. Cindy called it drab. "It won't take much," she said earnestly. "Just a little dab of lace at the neckline, maybe your something old? Or I have some white velvet roses, the really good kind, not the junk from the craft store. I could sort of arrange them—''

"No."

"You'll need something borrowed, and they'd look super at the waist. You probably wouldn't even need to bother with a bouquet."

Steff rolled her eyes, and Cindy flushed. She knew what they all thought of her hats, even though she'd explained they were only working designs and that the real models, when she could afford to make them, would be far more beautiful "I just thought I'd offer to...you know. Help perk it up a bit."

It was probably fortunate that Aunt S. called upstairs at that moment. "Cin-*dee!*"

"Yes, ma'am, I'm coming."

It was Charlie again. He hadn't been invited, but his mother, lacking a baby-sitter, had brought him along anyway. Cindy was right on his heels as he went whooping and hollering down the front stairs. Charlie was quick as a weasel, out the front door before she could grab onto his shirttail.

"Go on outside and don't come in again until he's thoroughly worn out," ordered Aunt S., who was of the children-should-be-seen-and-not-heard school of child-rearing.

Cindy's sympathies were with Charlie. She'd been only slightly older than he was now when she'd first met her courtesy aunt. Old enough to recognize a dragon in a black silk dress, but not old enough to deal with one. Little had changed since then.

They played ball until Charlie smacked one into the rose garden, then they switched to guess what color car passes by next. It was a slow game. At this time of day, there wasn't much traffic.

"Hey, a squirrel! I'm gonna catch him and put him in a box and take him home!"

"Charlie, leave that animal alone, he's got teeth that can—*Charlie!*"

The car came around the curve so fast there was no time to think. Cindy practically flew forward, tackling the heedless child and rolling them both into the azalea hedge across the street.

"Idiot! You blooming idiot!" she screeched at the driver of the luxury car, which had swerved to the curb and come to a tire-squealing stop. Breathless, she was still sprawled across Charlie's body when the car door swung open and one long, khaki-clad leg emerged.

"Hey, you're squashing me," Charlie protested. At least he was still in one piece. Just to be sure, she quickly felt his arms and legs before allowing him to squirm away from her. "You wait right there. Don't you dare move an inch from this spot," she warned, and such was her tone of voice that the child gulped and nodded.

"But you scared that old squirrel away," he accused. Pale, on the verge of tears, he was determined not to let on how frightened he was.

Cindy, still on her hands and knees, was torn between hugging him and shaking some sense into him. "Good thing I did," she growled. "He'd have bitten your finger off and likely died of food poisoning."

Struggling stiffly to her feet, she caught her breath as pain sliced through her from an assortment of minor ailments. Gravelly asphalt and hard, rocky earth weren't exactly kind to tender flesh, even when wearing jeans. She'd raked the skin off both knees and the heels of both hands.

"You little fool, don't you know any better than to run out into the street without looking?" a man's voice said. "Wait—don't move, you might be hurt."

Fear caught up with Charlie and he began to sob just as Cindy opened her mouth to let fly with a few choice phrases. She closed it again in deference to tender young ears. Charlie didn't need his already impressive vocabulary expanded. Fortunately she'd had years of practice in the art of swallowing her temper.

The reckless fool from the car had his hands on her thigh. "Stop that! Don't you know any better than to drive like a bat out of he—heck in a residential neighborhood?" Eyes blazing, she went to shove him away.

"Stand still. Oh, God, your hands are bleeding." Manacling her wrists, he lifted them for a closer look.

Cindy peered at her stinging palms, then lifted accusing eyes to his face. "You were—"

Oh, no. Oh, please no, not him!

"You're right. I was driving too fast. I'm sorry."

"Don't tell me, tell that poor child you nearly ran down!"

"Can you bend your knee?"

She'd already flexed both knees. They stung like the very devil, but at least they both worked.

"You didn't hit your head, did you?" He had the kind of voice that ought to be labeled hazardous to a woman's health. Or her whatever. It set off nerves she didn't even know she had, and that was saying a lot, because at the moment most of her nerves were busy registering acute pain.

Charlie was sniffling, clinging to her thigh and wiping his nose on the leg of her jeans. She gave the star of a thousand daydreams one long, glowering look and jerked her hands free of his grasp.

This was *not* the way she'd planned it. She'd planned to be wearing her yellow cotton, with her hair in a French braid, with eye shadow and lipstick and enough powder to disguise her freckles.

Instead she was standing here in thin, worn out jeans, every trembling cell in her body awash with pain and embarrassment, not to mention fright and the dregs of an ancient crush. "Oh…blast!" she cried. Sweeping Charlie up in her arms, she marched across the street, leaving John Hale Hitchcock staring after her.

Actually, march didn't exactly describe it. Charlie was a lot heavier than he looked, and her hip hurt. She'd already given it a good workout what with the wedding and all the extra work and chasing after Charlie. A five-yard dash followed by a flying tackle hadn't helped matters.

Hitch stared after the woman he'd nearly run down. Something about that wild red hair and that stubborn little chin snagged at his memory, but he couldn't quite place her. Not too surprising, since it had been years since he'd last visited Mocksville. She'd royally chewed him out, and with just cause. He had been speeding. The signs said 35. He'd been doing at least 45. The stop-off at his parents' place still had his gut tied in knots. After all these years, you'd think he'd have learned how to deal with the doubts, the frustrated feeling of being a kid who'd done something unforgivable. The feeling that he was somehow responsible for the fact that his parents would rather retreat to their separate studies than spend five minutes with their only son.

One of these days he'd wise up and stop trying. They had his phone number, in case they should ever want to reach him.

Hitch sat in the car for several minutes, still shaken, before starting the engine and creeping the remaining few yards to the MacCollums' driveway. He owed the little firebrand an apology. If she hadn't been right on the kid's heels when he burst out of the hedge, Hitch would have struck him, sure as the world. It was a wonder he hadn't hit them both, driving with his mind on other matters. At that speed, he'd have passed right by Mac's place without even slowing down.

He'd have to check on her later, to be sure she wasn't seriously hurt. She'd been limping when she'd disappeared into the Stephensons' house next door. Mac might know who she was—a pint-size redhead with blazing blue eyes and a tongue like a whipsaw. A wedding guest, maybe. Possibly a baby-sitter. Whoever she was, she deserved a proper apology, and before he left town he would see that she got one.

A day later, Hitch was actually beginning to unwind. In the process of putting in a couple of killer years trying to get his business up and running, he'd nearly forgotten how to relax.

The MacCollums taught him all over again. No way could anyone stand on ceremony in a house that was casual to the point of sloppiness, in which meals were taken in the big family kitchen with everyone wanting to know all about his business, and what it was, exactly, that an industrial engineer did, and how his folks, who lived in Lynchburg, Virginia, were getting along. And incidentally, when he was going to settle down and raise a family. Knowing that the MacCollums' interest was prompted by genuine caring, Hitch couldn't resent it.

The friendly inquisition eased off whenever a friend or neighbor would drop in. Someone would bring over a watermelon or a bucket of tomatoes or a basket of figs, and talk would shift to the wedding and Mac's ski resorts, and where the happy couple planned to live.

Mac spent as much time as possible at the Stephensons' house with his fiancée. The poor guy was besotted. Steff spent considerably less time at the MacCollums' place. Hitch wished them both well, but didn't hold out much hope for a long and happy union.

"Who's the redhead next door?" he asked Mac after the last straggler had left. "If I remember correctly, Mary—or Marnie?—had dark hair."

"You mean Maura. Yeah, she does, only she's got it all streaked up with blond now. Ask me, it was better the way it was, but you know women."

Actually, Hitch didn't. At least, not beyond a certain point. "Redhead. About yea high." He gestured appropriately. "Blue eyes a size too big for her face, freckles, pointed chin, tongue like a machete."

Mac chuckled. "You must've tangled with Cindy. She's been in high gear ever since Mrs. S. talked Steff into having a simple home wedding instead of using the church and the club."

From the level of activity next door, all the vans coming and going, *simple* was the last word Hitch would have used to describe it. "Cindy who? Cindy what?"

"Danbury. Lorna Stephenson was a Danbury before she was married, so I guess Cindy's some sort of cousin or something. Came to live with them when she was only a kid."

"That's why she looked so familiar," Hitch mused. "I don't think I ever actually met her until yesterday, when I nearly ran her down in the street." He went on to describe the brief encounter.

"You wouldn't have met her, she was only a kid back then, not old enough to hang around our gang. Besides, Mrs. S. kept her pretty busy. Still does. I like Cindy, she makes me laugh, and you know me—I can always use a good yuk."

Cindy. If Hitch had ever heard her name, he couldn't remember it. He wondered how old she was. Doing a bit of swift mental arithmetic, he figured she was at least twenty, maybe more. At first glance he'd taken her for a kid, but when she'd raised that heart-shaped little face, so pale her freckles stood out like rust spots, and sizzled him with a blast from a pair of laser blue eyes, he'd realized she was older than she looked.

"Yeah, well...I owe her an apology. Maybe I'll get a chance to speak to her Saturday during the festivities."

Chapter Two

At the groom's house, the prewedding festivities went on from morning until night, from casual drop-in breakfast guests to late-night beery reminiscences. The friendly, easygoing MacCollums knew everyone in town. Pop MacCollum had been the high school football coach and Mama Mac, as she was called, a retired school teacher, was the woman people came to when they needed help, or sympathy, or simply a nonjudgmental ear.

At first Hitch, still uptight after the visit with his own parents, followed by the near miss with the redhead and the kid, had found ways of avoiding the convivial mob scene. By the second day he had unwound to the point where he was actually beginning to enjoy himself. Or at least to enjoy Mac's enjoyment. The groom-to-be was having the time of his life, being the envy of all his male friends for having landed the most gorgeous woman in three counties.

At least they claimed to envy him, Hitch thought cynically, and it would never occur to Mac to doubt their sincerity.

At the moment, a leisurely game of croquet was under way. Maura, Hitch observed from his lawn chair in the shade of a giant magnolia, wasn't above nudging the ball with her foot. Steff, resplendent in white silk slacks, a white silk shirt and white, high-heeled sandals, was better at striking a pose than at actually playing the game.

Mac's besotted gaze followed her as she moved into the sunlight, which made her pale blond hair glimmer like a halo. "She's sure something, isn't she? I still can't believe she's gonna be mine."

"Yeah, she's something." Without being specific, Hitch would allow that much. "Where's Cindy?"

"Who? Oh, is that still buggin' you? Hey, don't sweat it, man, Cindy never held a grudge in her life."

"All the same, I owe her an apology and I always pay my debts."

"Know what I think?" Mac was on his third beer at half past two on a sweltering August afternoon. "I think you've developed a thing for freckle-faced redheads in your old age," he teased. Mac had always been one to tease, but thanks to his unfailing good nature, no one ever took offense.

"What I've developed," Hitch growled, a reluctant grin taking the edge off, "is a guilty conscience. I came down pretty hard on her, and she was completely blameless. If she hadn't dived after that kid I could've hit him. I really would like to apologize and get it off my chest."

"Man, don't take it so serious. Cindy's used to people yelling at her. Not that Miz S. ever actually yells, but that woman can pack a wallop without even raising her voice."

Hitch replaced his empty bottle in the wire holder beside his chair. "Like mother, like daughter, they say. It's not too late to back out."

Mac sighed. "Yeah, it is. It was too late the day Steff was born. She was made for me, man, only I've had the devil of a time convincing her."

Suddenly, Hitch straightened. "There she is now," he muttered, easing his six-foot-two frame up from the low lounge chair.

Cindy spotted her target and hurried across the lawn. "Steff, you're wanted on the phone. It's Wade, about your hair appointment."

"Well, where is it?"

"Where is—oh, the portable. I guess someone left it out in the back yard and the batteries ran down. Either that or Charlie got hold of it."

"Oh, for pity's sake," the elegant blonde exclaimed.

"Problem?" inquired a quiet baritone voice.

Cindy whirled, her hip locked and she stumbled. Hitch reached out to steady her and she yanked her arm free. It was bad enough just seeing him again, so close she could see the squint lines at the corners of his slate-gray eyes, the few silver strands scattered through his thick, dark hair.

Feeling the warmth of his hard palm on her arm, it was as if someone had suddenly flushed a covey of quail where her heart was supposed to be.

She managed to say "No problem," as she stepped back from the path through the hedge between the two houses and waited for Steff to precede her.

And waited. Phone call evidently forgotten, Steff was gazing up at Hitch through her long eyelashes and touching her hair in that way she had that Cindy, no matter how she practiced before a mirror, had never been able to accomplish.

At least, not with the same results.

"Go back and tell Wade the appointment stands," she directed.

"I'll tell him," Cindy said doubtfully, "but he said if you can possibly put it off until Saturday morning—"

"Tell him I can't, that I'm getting married Saturday, and my rehearsal ball is Friday night, and if he doesn't do my hair Friday afternoon he'll be sorry."

Hitch heard it all, tried to withhold judgment for Mac's sake and watched the little redhead's slender shoulders rise and fall in defeat. He pitied Wade. Whoever the guy was, whatever he'd done, he was going to pay through the nose for it.

Hitch told himself if he was any sort of friend at all, he would kidnap this blond witch and hold her hostage until Mac came to his senses.

"Wait a minute, will you, Cindy?" he said when his red-haired quarry headed back through the hedge.

"Don't have time, I left the iron on." She had her own style of haughty, and it made Steff look like a rank amateur.

"I won't take but a minute of your valuable time," he said before he could check the sarcasm.

But she was gone, and he refused to chase after any woman.

Maura was strolling over to join them. Steff waved her away, sighed and touched her hair again. "Croquet is such a childish game, isn't it? I don't know why I bother." Her Southern accent took on a finishing-school polish, which was absurd considering the school she'd attended, Salem College, was just over in the next county.

Hitch heard the Stephensons' side door close quietly. Another opportunity missed. Dammit, he didn't know why he even bothered. As soon as Mac told him who she was, he should have gone over there, spoken his piece, and by now it would be over and forgotten.

Well...maybe not forgotten. Snatches of the past were beginning to return. A redheaded waif watching wistfully from the sidelines like a kid outside a candy store window. He'd given her no more than a passing thought at the time, but now he wondered why she'd never been included.

Because she'd been just a kid? She wasn't that much younger than Steff and Maura. Probably just naturally shy.

But it hadn't been shyness he'd glimpsed in those blazing eyes. There'd been fear, followed swiftly by anger that first time. And pain? Yeah, that, too. He'd mentioned her limp to Mac, afraid her mad dive to escape his wheels had caused it, but Mac told him she'd always had a slight limp, especially when she'd been overdoing.

Evidently, she'd been overdoing.

Forget her, man. You told her you were sorry just after it happened. Let it go.

We're on the final countdown, Cindy thought gleefully as she dashed up the back stairs carrying an armload of clean towels and a heavy tea tray. She was sorely tempted to tell Charlie's mother, a second cousin whose husband owned a bank or something, that towels could be used more than once without laundering, and that there was a perfectly good kettle and a supply of tea bags in the kitchen.

Tonight was the rehearsal party. Tomorrow was the wedding, and then, glory hallelujah, it would all be over. The guests would go home, Aunt S. would leave for the mountains to recuperate, Steff and Mac would be off on their honeymoon, Maura would be getting ready to head north and conquer New York.

And as soon as she got her car running again, little Cindy would be free to go back to her regular Monday job. The job that actually paid cash instead of just room and board. Another six months and she should have reached her savings goal, if a new alternator didn't cost too much, and then it would be goodbye Mocksville, hello world!

A few minutes later, after freeing a snagged zipper, collecting a bundle of lingerie to hand wash, a trayful of dirty dishes and an empty pizza box from the room Steff's friends shared, she headed down the front stairway—the back one was so steep she avoided it whenever she could, even though Aunt S. always frowned to see her coming down into the front hall with a load of laundry or dirty dishes.

"Hi," someone called softly when she was half-way down. Her carefully balanced load tilted precariously.

"Steff's not here, but I think Maura might be around somewhere." Maura was always around somewhere if there was a chance of seeing Hitch. Cindy had heard them talking about him last night—Steff, Maura and Steff's girlfriends. The consensus was that he was a real catch, a certified hunk and sexier than what's-his-name who had starred in that hit movie that Cindy had never got around to seeing.

She could have added her own opinion, but she didn't think it would be appreciated.

"Watch it—here, let me take that tray."

"I've got it," she said, and grudgingly added her thanks.

"You need a dumbwaiter."

It stumped her for a second, but then she blinked and said, "Oh, you mean one of those elevator gadgets. If they come in mahogany with stained glass windows, I might get Aunt S. to have one installed. She doesn't care for modern conveniences."

"But then, she's not the one being inconvenienced, is she?"

Cindy couldn't help herself. Her eyes sparkled, her lips twitched and she bit back an irreverent retort. Hitch was grinning openly. Had anyone mentioned that he had gorgeous teeth?

And a sense of humor?

Would that crew even recognize, much less appreciate, a sense of humor?

She knew in explicit detail what they thought of his narrow behind and his broad shoulders, and the way his slacks rode low at his waist and sort of bunched up at the fly. Maura said she'd seen him in swim trunks, and he more than lived up to his advertising.

They'd all groaned and then giggled—even Steff, who wasn't a giggler, and who shouldn't be thinking that way about her fiancé's best man.

Cindy, who'd been delivering another round of diet colas at the time, was tempted to mention his nasty disposition and his recklessness behind the wheel, but she'd learned a long time ago to keep her opinions to herself.

"I've been wanting to talk to you about what happened the other day," he said when she reached the bottom step.

At close range he was even more lethal than he was behind the wheel of a car. Funny how she could remember so much about him after all these years. Such as the way he'd always been so patient with the pesky kids from across the street. Such as the way he'd always risen whenever Mama Mac came into a room.

Such as the way all the girls, herself included, had been in love with him then. Not that he'd ever even noticed her.

And while the intervening years might not have improved his driving skills, they'd done nothing but enhance his dark good looks. Fortunately, Cindy had long ago outgrown her brief infatuation, since the days when she used to gaze at him through the hedge whenever Mac brought him home from college.

"Look, I'm sorry, but I really don't have time to

talk now. Besides, there's nothing to talk about. You're a rotten driver, and I'm lucky as the dickens, and that's the end of that, okay?''

"Not okay. I'm usually an exemplary driver, but—''

"No excuses, I told you I don't have time.'' She edged past him and headed for the kitchen.

He was two steps behind her. Where in the world was Maura? she wondered. Where was everyone else? Usually, the house was brimming with people, all with their separate demands. "Shouldn't you be practicing your role as Mac's best man?''

"Tonight's the rehearsal.'' The festivities were being held immediately following the rehearsal instead of after the ceremony, as the bride and groom had to leave right after the wedding to make their connections to Bermuda. "Tell you what, save me a dance at the party afterward and we'll call it even.''

She gave him an exasperated look that in Hitch's estimation did nothing at all to diminish the effect of those steady blue eyes. "I never—''

"Never say never.'' Hitch's smile, meant to be disarming, faltered as it occurred to him that she might not dance because she was self-conscious about her limp. He started to tell her it was barely noticeable, and thought better of it. "Look, we could just sit and talk, maybe share a glass of champagne and some cake—how about that?''

Cindy always hated it when people were embarrassed by her limp; otherwise, she seldom even thought about it. More often than not when people noticed they assumed she'd hurt her ankle, or had something in her shoe. Sometimes she said she had. It was no big deal. Didn't even bother her except when she was rushed off her feet, as she had been lately.

"I really do appreciate the offer, and there's nothing I'd like better, but I'll be far too busy to join the festivities. You wouldn't believe how much work is involved in a simple home wedding." And if that sounded condescending, then it was just too bad. It was a wonder she was able to put two coherent words together, the way he affected her brain.

"It's being handled by a professional, right?"

"Not even professionals can do everything." Especially not with Aunt S. second-guessing their every move and Steff constantly changing her mind about details.

"Caterers handling the rehearsal dinner?" he persisted. He happened to know the Macs were footing the bill, although there was no preventing Mrs. S. from running the show.

"We have a houseful of guests. They have to eat three meals a day—more like seven, if you count snacks. And then there's Charlie...."

"Oh, yeah, I do remember Charlie. How is he?"

"Still into everything, which is one more reason I'll be too busy to take you up on your kind offer. But thanks." Looking directly into his cool gray eyes, she smiled, confident she had handled the matter tactfully and efficiently, and that would be the end of that.

Mercy, it had better be! She couldn't take too many more up-close-and-personal encounters with John Hale Hitchcock.

* * *

With the end in sight, Cindy was fervently looking forward to the moment when everyone was busy dining and dancing downstairs and she could have the big old claw-footed tub to herself for more than five minutes. As large as the house was, there were only two and a half baths—none at all, of course, in the attic. She had plans for a long, peaceful, lilac-scented soak followed by an evening spent reading in bed while everyone else was downstairs partying.

Sheer, hedonistic luxury.

Steff poked her head into the laundry room where Cindy was folding sheets. "You put him up to it, didn't you?"

"Put who up to what?" The last time she'd seen Charlie he'd been pestering the caterer's helper for samples.

"As if you didn't know. He wants you to go to the party."

"Charlie?"

"Not Charlie, Hitch. He told Mama you'd promised him a dance."

There went her heart again, doing aerobics. "I did no such thing. Besides, I've got a date with a good book."

"Break it. You can put in a brief appearance without dancing. Tell him your feet hurt." For all her arrogance, Steff could be generous in her own careless way.

"Well, they do, but that's not the problem. I don't have anything to wear. I don't think Aunt S. would be real happy if I turned up in jeans and one of my fancy hats." She smiled, picturing her aunt's reaction. Still, it was nice to be invited, even if she had no intention of going.

"Look, I'll lend you a dress and you can sit on the sidelines. At least you'll be handy if one of us needs anything."

Oops. I smiled too quickly.

If Steff had genuinely wanted her there, Cindy might have considered going, but a grudging, last-minute invitation prompted by someone else…

"Thanks, Steff, but I'll pass if you don't mind."

"Oh, for heaven's sake, the last thing I need is to have Hitch and Mama on my back. Look, I'll pick out something you can wear and leave it on my bed. Now don't argue, I don't have time, and besides, you know how Mama is when things don't go according to her plans."

Oh, yes, Cindy knew how Mama was, all right. It was easier to go along than to argue. "Then thanks, I'll pick up the dress when I go upstairs next time."

"Great. Is my blue suit back from the cleaners?"

"In your closet. Do you want me to pack it?"

"No, on second thought, I don't think it's right for Bermuda. Pack the white linen, instead. It'll wrinkle, but they'll have maid service."

The gown was a sophisticated designer model with matching shoes that Steff had spent a fortune for several years ago. Complaining that the color made her look pasty, she'd worn it only a few times.

Cindy had a feeling the odd shade, somewhere between peach and ecru, wouldn't do much for her own complexion, either. Instead of basting up the

hem, which would have left marks, she shortened
the straps, gave up on the waistline and had just
slipped the garment over her head when Steff came
in to ask which suitcase her jewelry had been packed
in. "Speaking of jewelry, I guess you'll need something. You look sort of drab."

"A new car?"

Steff actually smiled. "Something smaller. Earrings, I guess. With all those freckles a necklace
would be wasted."

Thank you, ma'am, I really needed that.

"Try to do something with your hair, will you?
You should've made an appointment with Wade."

"Twenty-five bucks plus tip for a trim? No
thanks."

Her hair was impossible. She could French braid
it and within minutes, curly strands would work
loose. Hair spray only made it look like a fright wig.
"I could wear a hat," she said hopefully.

"Don't you dare." Cindy's hats were a joke
among the Stephensons, but she no longer took offense. One of these days, she promised herself. One
of these fine days...

It was Maura who provided the earrings. "Steff
said I had to lend you these. Don't you dare lose
them—they match my favorite ring." She tossed a
pair of sparkling diamond-and-pearl studs on the
dresser and left. Evidently she'd heard that Hitch
had had something to do with Cindy's being invited
to the party, and resented it.

As if Cindy would be any competition. Maura
wasn't in Steff's league when it came to looks, but

she had her own style of beauty. Compared to either of them, Cindy wasn't even in the running.

The earrings were for pierced ears. Cindy's weren't. Not wanting to make an issue of it, she returned them, leaving them on Maura's dresser beside her jewelry case, which was always kept locked.

Slipping on her tennis shoes, she hurried down the back stairs and out into the garden, cut two large pink roses and shaved off the thorns. Then, hiking her heavy satin skirt up over her knees, she dashed back upstairs and carefully fastened them to the French braid.

"At least no one can call you drab," she told her mirror image.

Not that anyone would even spare her a glance, with the likes of Steff and Maura and all their glamorous friends around. The house was already overflowing with men in penguin suits and women in every color of the rainbow, all sparkling and laughing and flirting.

Last of all, she stepped into the shoes that matched her gown. Taking a deep breath, she carefully held up her skirt to keep from tripping, and made her wobbly way down the front stairs, half expecting Aunt S. to confront her and send her back to her room.

Chapter Three

Madam S. was everywhere, keeping an eagle eye on the wedding party, the half dozen or so servants hired for the occasion and the invited guests, who started arriving before the rehearsal was even finished. Hitch actually found himself sympathizing with the woman, who had obviously taken on more than she'd bargained for by insisting on having both the wedding and the party—she called it a ball—at home. She'd have been better served to limit the size and scope, and then turn over full control to the professionals instead of trying to oversee every phase of the production personally.

He felt sorrier still for Mac, but then, after living next door to the dragon and her two fledgling dragonettes all his life, Mac knew what he was getting into. He might look like a harmless hayseed, but he was a lot sharper than most folks gave him credit for being...which often worked to his advantage.

Nothing like being underestimated to give a guy an edge.

The house was a large one, the living room, dining room and front parlor, empty of furniture, spacious. But the space was rapidly filling up with dancers, and the linen-draped buffet was under serious siege. The air conditioner had already surrendered. A few black ties had been tugged askew and several of the ladies were noticeably glowing.

Mac was having a ball. Literally. Even Steff had unbent enough to kick off her four-inch heels and dance.

Maura came up behind Hitch and tucked her hand in his arm. "Where are you going?"

"Forgot something," he improvised quickly. "Save me a dance later, will you?" He had to get out of here. The acoustics weren't designed for modern amplifiers. With everyone straining to talk over the band, the effect was deafening.

Intent on escaping to the cool, relatively quiet front porch, where a row of comfortable rocking chairs were aligned with mathematical precision, Hitch eluded the platinum-blond bridesmaid who'd been stalking him for the past two days. He made it as far as the foyer, and there was Cindy, halfway down the stairs.

Halting in his tracks, he stared up at the woman, who stared back. A stricken look on her face, she gripped the banister with one hand while the other clutched a fistful of gown that was too long, too loose and far too sophisticated. She reminded him of a little girl caught playing dress-up in her mama's best nightgown.

He edged closer to the stairway, afraid she was about to turn tail and run. "Cindy?" Should he grab her before she disappeared, or what?

Before he could make up his mind, she loosened her death grip on the stair rail, waggled a brave little three-finger salute in his direction and started down. Head held high, she even managed a shaky smile.

"Hi," he said softly as she neared the bottom. She was wearing high-heeled shoes with rhinestone clips that looked a couple of sizes too large. Like the gown. "I've been waiting for you."

Tactical error. Even in the dim light of the brass-and-crystal chandelier, he could see her color drain away, then rush back to stain her cheeks, all but obliterating her freckles.

And what the devil had she done to her hair? "You look lovely," he said gallantly.

In a strange way, she did, if you disregarded everything but the essential Cindy. And he was finding it easier all the time to do that.

"Thank you," she said gravely. "It sounds as if the party's already started. The invitations said eight."

"Nobody stands on ceremony these days."

"Aunt S. does."

"I believe the general was overrun by her own troops." He caught the flicker of a smile and tucked it away like a trophy. "You're late. I was afraid you weren't coming."

"There were several last minute things that needed taking care of."

"I'll just bet there were," Hitch said dryly. Over the past three days, while he'd been trying to get her alone to offer an official apology, he'd caught glimpses of her dashing after the kid, or rushing around carrying loaded trays or armloads of laundry, or flowers or dry cleaning. Never empty-handed, always on the run. He'd even seen her on a stepladder polishing windows.

He figured she'd be damned glad when this wingding was over.

Standing at the bottom of the stairs, he waited for her to descend the last few steps. After a deep breath, one that drew his attention to her small, high breasts, she resumed her progress. When she stood before him, she gazed up and smiled again, this time as if she meant it.

Hitch felt as if someone had bashed him in the chest. Could eyes actually change color? He happened to know hers were blue, but tonight they looked dark as midnight. He'd never even noticed her lashes before. They were remarkable. Pale, fully an inch long, thick as a boxwood hedge and transparent at the tips.

She was wearing lipstick in a shade that clashed with her red hair and clashed even more with the gown she was wearing. A couple of deep pink roses, already beginning to wilt, added to the conflict.

All in all, she was a fashion designer's nightmare.

"Do I look all right?"

"You look...perfect."

Even as he spoke the words, he realized they were true. She looked real and warm and nervous, and oddly dignified, and he felt an unexpected urge to sweep her up and take her off to a place where no one would laugh at her, or order her to fetch and carry until she was ready to drop.

"I believe this is our waltz, princess."

Cindy managed to tear her gaze away from his face, but there was no escaping that voice. Deep and warm and slightly raspy, it resonated in the most unexpected places. It was a dark brown velvet voice, with underlying glints of gold. Unbidden, her imagination took off on a flight of its own.

"Cindy? You promised me a dance?"

"Oh. I'm sorry, I was woolgathering. I do that a lot."

She stood there smelling of soap and shampoo and wilted roses, and Hitch waited for her to collect her thoughts. What an odd girl she was, he mused, but then immediately amended his thoughts. She was no girl. She might be small—and even he, who knew little about ladies' fashions, could see that she knew even less than he did. Yet there was a dignity and a maturity about her that was completely lacking in either of her far more fashionable cousins.

"Shall we?" He held out a hand as the band struck up another waltz. Mrs. S.'s orders, no doubt. No reggae or rock in her front parlor, please.

"I don't waltz."

"On account of your leg?" He would never have mentioned it if he thought she was self-conscious about it.

"Actually, it's my hip, not my leg. It catches sometimes, but only when I'm tired or I turn too fast."

"Then we'll take slow turns, no dips, and as you're probably tired from all the running around you've been doing, I promise to do most of the work." He gave her what he considered his most nonthreatening smile.

"I'll step all over your feet. I told you I don't waltz—I never learned how."

"Then we'll practice first. I think we can hear the music from the front porch, don't you?"

"We could probably hear it all the way to Smith Grove."

Grinning, Hitch led her outside. When she turned to him, obviously bracing herself for a dreaded task, he said, "Relax, I'm not going to bite you."

"I *am* relaxed," she said grimly.

"Tell you what, why don't I snag us a couple of glasses of champagne first? I'm usually a better dancer with a drink or two under my belt."

"I might throw up all over you. I'm awfully nervous."

"I'm also good at dodging. Stay here, don't move, I'll be right back."

As good as his word, he returned only minutes later with two glasses, half a bottle of champagne and a plate piled high with assorted unidentifiable finger sandwiches. "See if you can locate the peanut butter and jelly, will you?"

She laughed. She had a surprisingly nice laugh, even though it was a bit rusty, as if it didn't get too much exercise. "Just don't eat the caviar," she warned. "Aunt S. insisted on serving it, but she ordered a bargain brand that tastes awful."

"Never did care for it, myself. Smells fishy. Now, here's something that looks like mashed potatoes on a cracker with a pickle on top. That's probably pretty harmless.''

She laughed again. Hell, he'd have stood on his head and wiggled his ears if it would bring about that kind of a response. You wouldn't think a guy his age would be turned on by the sound of a woman's laughter.

"Chicken salad with olives and feta cheese. It's Frank's favorite.''

"Who's Frank?'' Hitch bit off half a crackerful.

"The caterer. He's really sweet.''

Uh-oh.

"I run errands sometimes for his wife when he's too busy to take her to town. Shanie lost her driver's license, but it wasn't her fault.''

"It never is,'' Hitch said dryly. All the same, he was relieved to hear that sweet Frank had a wife. It never occurred to him to wonder why it mattered.

While the band wrapped up "Moon River'' and followed it with a couple of Beatles hits, he and Cindy sampled various party foods, sipped domestic champagne and talked. He'd been right about one thing: the champagne did help put her at ease.

However, any sign of relaxation disappeared when he stood and held out his hand. "Time for my dance,'' he reminded her.

"Oh, my, do I have to?''

"You don't believe in flattering a guy, do you?''

"The ones I know don't need flattery.''

"Hey, we all do. It's a dog-eat-dog world out there.''

"Let's just get this over with, shall we?''

Hitch couldn't help himself, he had to laugh.

"Are you this tactful with everyone, or is it just me?"

"I flunked charm school. Come on, before I lose my nerve." She placed her small, damp palm in his hand and frowned down at her feet.

He slipped his other arm around her waist and tugged her gently against him. "Relax," he growled. "You need another sip of champagne?"

"I've already had two glasses."

"You're stiff as angle iron. Close your eyes, pretend you're half-asleep and just let yourself drift. Trust me."

She sighed. Her head flopped onto his chest. Her hair tickled his chin, and without thinking, he kissed the top of her head and began to sway in time with the music.

She swayed with him. After a while, he took a few steps, and she followed him perfectly. They weren't waltzing, but then, the band was no longer playing a waltz, so it was just as well.

She began to sing the words of an old Roberta Flack number. It always irritated him when his dancing partner sang along with the band. This time it didn't. When she got to the part about the earth moving under her feet, his arms tightened around her. He couldn't help himself. He felt a mixture of amusement, tenderness and protectiveness, and for the life of him, he couldn't say why.

She broke off and apologized. "Aunt S. hates it when I sing."

"Aunt S. is a cheerless dragon."

It was Cindy's turn to chuckle. "I think I'm actually dancing, aren't I? Have I stepped on your toes yet?''

''You can't tell?''

''I wasn't sure. I stuffed toilet paper in the toes of these shoes, so I can't feel much there. Or maybe it's the wine. I never drink wine. You can probably guess why.''

''No, actually I can't, but while you're in this mellow frame of mind, let me get something off my chest.''

She lifted her head, and he pulled it back, pressing her cheek against said chest. It felt good there. As if it belonged. ''I was driving at least ten miles over the limit, maybe more than that. My mind was on something else, and if you hadn't rushed out when you did and shoved the kid out of the way, I hate to think of what could have happened.''

''You don't have to—''

''Let me finish. I was in the wrong and I handled it badly. If you want the truth, I was scared, only it came out as anger.''

''You don't have to explain. I was scared, too, and I yelled at you. Sometimes I have trouble with my temper.''

''No kidding.''

This time when she lifted her head it was to grin at him. She'd eaten off half her lipstick. He was tempted to—

No, he wasn't.

''So, tell me, Miss Danbury, what do you do for entertainment?''

''I have a job.''

He stopped moving to stare down at her. "You have a what?"

"Well, it's not really a job, but you see, on my days off—that's always on a Monday—I have this little service thing called Send Cindy."

Her day off. Since when did a person take a day off from family?

But then, he'd taken more than a day off from his—he'd taken years. "Go on," he prompted. "I'm interested."

The band segued into "Moon River" again. Their repertoire was rather limited. Fireflies twinkled in the mock orange bushes, and from a distance came the plaintive call of a whippoorwill.

"You see, Uncle Henry gave me a car for my birthday before he died. Since I don't have another source of income, and I—"

"You don't have a what?"

"Well, I hardly need it, since Aunt S. gives me room and board and pays for my six-month checkup at the dentist, and Maura and Steff keep me supplied with clothes. Their shoes don't fit me, but the discount stores have really nice shoes cheap, and I've got my savings for emergencies."

Hitch was pretty sure it was the champagne that had loosened her tongue. He had a feeling she'd regret her artless confidences tomorrow, if she even remembered them.

He sort of hoped she would remember, at least part of tonight. The part where he held her in his arms, and they swayed together under the yellow bug-light on the old-fashioned front porch, dodging rocking chairs and out-of-alignment boards, surrounded by the intoxicating scent of whatever was blooming out there.

"So...this business of yours. Tell me about it."

"You have to promise not to tell Aunt S. She'd have a fit if she knew I was getting paid for running errands for some of her best friends."

"She doesn't know?"

Cindy shook her head against his chest. The spicy scent of crushed roses drifted up to tickle his senses. "Honestly, I didn't ask them not to tell her, but they sort of understood...I think. You see, I started out using a bicycle years and years ago—picking up things from the drugstore, and library books, that sort of thing. But once Uncle Henry gave me a car I branched out. Like on Mondays I drive Miss Emma to the beauty parlor for her shampoo, color rinse and set, and while she's in there, I do Mrs. Harris's grocery shopping, and after that, there's Arvilla Davis's cages to clean. She loves her birds, but she hates cleaning the cages. And then, sometimes two or three of them get together and I drive them to Hanes Mall over in Winston for lunch and shopping."

Cindy leaned back in his arms and gazed up at him, her eyes mysterious pools in her pale face. "It's not much, but I charge by the hour, and it pays for my car expenses and lets me save for the future, only now I have to have a new alternator, unless Mikey down at the garage can find me a used one. At any rate, it's not a real career, it's only a means to an end."

She broke off to catch her breath. "Oh, my, I talk too much, don't I? It must be the champagne, because usually I don't. Talk, that is. I mean, not all this much.''

It was the champagne. Now that he had her at a disadvantage he was tempted to lead her into further disclosures. Being his parents' son, he had learned a thing or two about leading a witness.

Being a gentleman, he refrained. She was too vulnerable. And as tempted as he was, he couldn't do it.

Well, hell.

Chapter Four

Hours later Hitch lay awake in his bed, arms crossed under his head, and thought about the situation next door. According to Mac, the Stephensons were well off. Henry Stephenson had worked hard, invested well and lived frugally—or as frugally as the father of two extravagant daughters can live—in the house he'd inherited from his parents. Cindy was a Danbury, a sort of stepniece to Mrs. S., as Mac had explained it.

What the devil was a stepniece? Either she was or she wasn't.

In which case, why didn't any of the widow Stephenson's wealth filter down to the youngest member of the family?

Next question: Cindy had referred to her Monday job as a means to an end. What end? Finding herself a rich husband? That would've been both her cousins' goal, although Steff could probably have done better for herself than Mac. At least financially. Hitch would like to believe she'd finally seen beneath Mac's freckles and his Howdy-Doody grin to the solid gold core underneath, but only time would tell.

At least he now knew why Cindy had been wearing a gown that was all wrong for her strong coloring and delicate beauty. It was a hand-me-down. Steff's probably. Maura went in for bolder colors, but as a blonde, Steff favored pastels.

Some redheads might have been able to get away with wearing faded orange satin, but not Cindy. And definitely not with wilted pink roses and whatever shade her lipstick had been.

Tomorrow, he thought as he drifted off, was the big day. After that, he'd be out of here. Gradually, sleep relaxed the muscles of his face, all but a slight frown that carried over into his dreams.

The wedding was almost an anticlimax. Steff looked as if she had a headache, and even Mac was without his usual easy grin. A few cases of domestic champagne would do that, Hitch mused, hoping Cindy wasn't regretting last night's indulgence too much.

But the happy pair did the deed, then stood patiently between the potted palms while the wedding guests, numbering thirty-nine of their most intimate friends and close family, showered them with best wishes and ribald advice.

Hitch made a point of searching out Cindy, finally locating her near the door. There were shadows around her eyes and the collar of her blue linen dress was rucked up in the back as if she'd gotten dressed in a hurry, but at least she was present. And she was smiling. Tears glistened on her cheeks, but her smile was the brightest thing in the room, to his way of thinking.

Although he still couldn't figure out why she wasn't one of the attendants. Maura was the maid of honor, and the other two were old classmates of Steff's, but why not three? Why not Cindy? Even Madam S. had got in on the act by giving her daughter away.

It was then that Hitch made up his mind to take advantage of the MacCollums' invitation to stay over a few more days to help them get over losing their only son. Pop had been halfway joking, of course. He liked the idea of having a beautiful daughter. But Mama Mac had quietly repeated that old saw about a daughter being a daughter all her life, but a son being a son until he takes him a wife.

Hitch knew one thing for sure. If Cindy had belonged to the MacCollums instead of the Stephensons, they'd have treasured her and she would have enriched their lives a thousandfold.

It took a while for things to settle down. Mac and Steff left shortly after the ceremony for the airport in Greensboro, in a flurry of tin cans, balloons and soaped car windows. On Sunday morning Mrs. S. left for Roaring Gap with a friend to recuperate, and Maura girded her loins for one last shopping marathon before heading north.

"Why not wait and shop in New York?" Hitch

asked Cindy. He'd wandered over to see if he could help restore order.

"I wondered about it, too, but she said she needs decent clothes to wear for shopping in New York."

He shook his head. Cindy smiled and went on picking wilted blossoms from a crystal vase of white glads, and trimming the stems. "Did you come to say goodbye?"

Allowing himself the pleasure of watching her deft hands at work, he said, "Matter of fact, I came to say hello. I've been invited to stay on a few days. It's been so long since I took a vacation I've almost forgotten how, but I thought I'd give it a try."

She went on working. He went on looking. Even wearing jeans that were a size too large, she had a neat posterior. Her waist was hidden under a baggy T-shirt, but he had an excellent memory of the way she'd felt when he'd held her against him.

Fragile, but decidedly feminine.

"Imagine that," she marveled softly. "A thrilling vacation in exotic Mocksville, only a few miles away from the muddy Yadkin River and within sight, if you climb the right tree, of the Brushy Mountains."

"You don't like Mocksville?"

"Actually, I do. It's a nice town and the people are really friendly, but there's not a whole lot going on here. At least, Steff and Maura always said it was dull as cornmeal. That's why Maura's going to New York."

"And you? What are you going to do now?"

Cindy was silent for so long he thought she wasn't going to reply, but then she said, "Well, there's my job. My Monday job, that is. I might be able to take on another day or so once Maura leaves and there are only the two of us left.''

Evidently she'd managed to get a few hours of rest last night, because her limp was nowhere in evidence. She had a quick, graceful way of moving that intrigued him. As a design engineer, he was always looking for ways to combine grace with efficiency, utility with beauty.

Cindy made it all seem so effortless.

''It's your turn,'' she said, handing him a dripping cut glass vase and a linen towel. ''Tell me about your work. Mac says you're some kind of an engineer, but I forgot which kind.''

Hitch carefully dried the Waterford vase, thinking that if his parents could see him at this moment, they'd be horrified. ''Industrial design. Ideally, we try to combine esthetics with function.'' It occurred to him that she herself was the perfect example, but she wasn't ready to hear it, and he damn sure wasn't about to say it.

Instead, he went on to describe what it was that his small firm of designers did. ''Primarily, we make everyday products more desirable by improving the appearance to appeal to a certain targeted market.''

She held up a cast aluminum juicer that had been around for at least half a century. ''This is ugly, but it still works better than any of the fancier ones I've tried. I'd buy it in a minute.''

''Why are we hanging out in the kitchen, talking about juicers?'' he asked suddenly, unfolding his length from the kitchen stool he'd been perched on.

''I'm redoing the flowers and putting away the

vases we don't need anymore. I don't know what you're doing here. Why don't you go out and—and play croquet or something?''

"Got a better idea. Why don't we both skip out for the day? How about a picnic at that park by the river—what's it called, Tanglefoot?''

"Tanglewood.'' She cast a helpless look at the potted palm and flower arrangements still to be dealt with.

"They'll wait.''

She had a wicked smile, a truly wicked smile, he decided. First her eyes lit up like candles, then a dimple flickered in one cheek. Then came the smile. It blew him away.

The park was crowded, but they found a shady place well off the beaten track where they could catch a glimpse of sunlight sparkling on a nearby duck pond. Hitch wondered what the devil he was doing there. He hated picnics. If he weren't careful he might set up expectations he had no intention of filling, and that would be a damn shame.

Cindy spread a patchwork quilt over the grass under the shade of an oak tree. "You're supposed to sit on it,'' she said when he just stood there holding the basket of leftover wedding food.

By the time she had him and everything else arranged to suit her, with the basket between them and the tree behind him in case he needed support, he had his defenses securely locked in place. He would give her this day, he told himself, because she'd earned it. Throughout this whole production she'd worked harder than anyone else, and had less to show for it. Steff had a truckload of trousseau and a gem of a husband. Together, they'd accumulated a whole slew of wedding gifts. Both bridesmaids had been given gold charm bracelets, and at least one had snared herself a new love interest. Maura, at least until she moved on to greener pastures, had taken over the coveted corner bedroom with its own bathroom, which had been Steff's.

As for Cindy, she'd been given the privilege of slipping into the parlor at the last minute to watch the actual ceremony. Once the other members of the family went their separate ways, she'd been left behind to clean up after them and put everything back in order.

But not today. Today would be his gift to her. It wasn't enough, but it would let him leave with a clear conscience. They'd start with the picnic and wind up the day with dinner at the best restaurant in town.

With that worthy end in mind, Hitch helped her devour the country ham sandwiches she'd insisted on making, the white chocolate brownies left over from the wedding, and the iced tea she'd packed in the cooler. They talked about everything under the sun. He was increasingly fascinated by the way her mind worked.

"*Hats?* You want to become a *hat designer?* That's the end you were talking about the other night?"

"I am a hat designer. A good one, too," she said proudly.

"Honey, designing a product is just the first step. Actually going into production is something else. It takes connections and a lot of business savvy, not to mention a bundle of money.''

She licked a streak of mustard off her top lip. Distracted, he lost the thread of conversation and picked it up again as she was saying, "I know it's not going to be easy. I can't draw very well, and I have to see a design in three dimensions. I don't have time to get a business education, and I don't have a whole lot of money. There's raw materials to buy—mostly I use cheap stuff for mock-up models, but every now and then I see genuine fake flowers on sale. Silk and velvet ones. I buy as many as I can afford, but right now I'm just trying to save enough to move into a place where I'll have room to work.''

"Why move? Why not stay where you are and save the rent?''

"There's barely room in the attic to get dressed, much less to work. Besides, Aunt S. hates my mess. She says it makes dust, and she's allergic.'' A pensive look stole over Cindy's delicate features, shadowing her expressive eyes. "Well, that's not entirely true. I mean, it is, but I'm ashamed to say that the real reason is that I want to leave before Aunt S. comes to depend on me even more than she does now. I know it's selfish, because she's given me a home all these years, but she's not getting any younger, and if she gets sick, or even thinks her health is failing, I'll never get away. I couldn't just move out and leave her if she truly needed me, and Maura plans to be a New York model, so you see, it's now or never. I think it's called a window of opportunity.''

Right. Maura was going to be a model. She had the requisite arrogance, if little else. Steff had snared herself a manageable husband with a promising future, and Cindy was selfishly going to try for a life of her own.

She toyed with a melting ice cube in her glass. "You think I'm being ungrateful, don't you? I am, I know it, but—"

"I think you might be somewhat impractical, but not ungrateful. Seems to me you've earned the right to live your own life. If your mind's made up, then I'd say a clean break's the best way to go."

He'd found it to be true in his own case, but then by the time he'd parted ways with his own family he'd had a lot more experience. He'd also had the security of a scholarship and some pretty solid prospects on down the line.

"I think so, too," she said gravely. "And of course, I'd stay in touch. If she needed me for anything, I'd always go back and help out, but if I have a place of my own, maybe a garage apartment in Winston-Salem, I wouldn't have to stay."

Without intending to, Hitch found himself telling her about his rocky relationship with his parents. It wasn't something he talked about, not even with Mac.

She listened as if she were taking it all in, and then said, "It's not that they're disappointed in you, Hitch, it's just that they had different dreams. Everybody has dreams. Mac says you used to draw pictures of radical cars and airplanes, and even furniture. He thinks you're some kind of genius. He said he'd never have passed half his courses at Tech without you."

"Yeah, well…Mac's bailed me out a time or two. He's good with people. That's never been one of my particular skills."

"Excuse me if I don't believe you. I watched the way Maura and Steff's bridesmaids hung all over you, like they didn't want to miss a single pearl that fell from your lips. You seemed to be enjoying it." Her tone was still solemn, but her eyes held a teasing twinkle.

"Looks can be deceiving."

"Steff promised Anna that since Maura was leaving, she'd try to fix her up with you."

"She's the one with the fingernails, right?" They were fire-engine red and about an inch and a half long. If the woman had had a serious thought in her head, it wasn't apparent.

"She seems nice, though—and she's from Virginia."

"I'm sure she is nice, but no thanks. I'll pass."

"I hate matchmaking, too," Cindy refilled their glasses and reached for another half sandwich— smoked turkey this time. Hitch picked up the other half. "Maura and Steff used to fix me up with dates until I put my foot down. I think I can do better on my own if I ever have time to try it."

"Sure you can." Funny, he'd never thought of her going out with another man. For some reason, he didn't particularly like thinking about it now.

"I'm not looking for Prince Charming, just someone decent who won't try to—oh, well, it's not going to happen anytime soon because I'll be too busy.''

Hitch set aside her tea glass, reached for the wine he'd brought along and filled two plastic flutes. She accepted one, sniffed it, sipped it and leaned back on her elbows.

She sighed. They watched as the sun sank behind the dusty, somnolent trees. Without intending to, Hitch found himself confiding a few of his own disastrous dating experiences. ''I ended up with a flat wallet, a shirt full of tears and mascara, and an impressive shiner, but I learned something about diplomacy. Remember that old saw about nothing ventured, nothing lost? I seldom venture anymore.''

''I think that's supposed to be nothing ventured, nothing gained,'' Cindy said dryly. Feeling as if she were drifting on a featherbed under the canopy of shady green leaves, she waved away a curious dragonfly and told Hitch about her most recent date. ''He was—what's that word? A dork? No, I guess he was just an ordinary jerk. Anyway, I might not be rich or pretty, but I deserve better than that.''

Carefully setting his wineglass aside, Hitch reached for hers and placed it on the grass beside the quilt. He lifted her hand and brought it up to his lips, kissed each knuckle and then turned her hand so that he could kiss the calluses at the base of each finger.

''Oh, my mercy, you don't have to do that,'' she whispered, mortified. ''No matter how much lotion I slather on, they're still rough as pine bark, and my nails...'' Her nails were clipped almost to the quick, but not chewed. There was a neat hairline of white showing at the end of each small, pink fingernail. "I tried the artificial kind, but I glued them on crooked and they kept snagging on everything, so I gave up."

She said it so earnestly, Hitch didn't know whether to laugh or sympathize. So he did neither. Instead, he leaned over and kissed her lightly on the forehead, on the tip of her nose and then on the lips.

Lightly. No matter how much he was tempted to linger, to explore this unlikely friendship that had sprung up between them, he knew better than to encourage anything more. Nothing ventured, nothing lost, he reminded himself.

"Friends?" he said softly.

Solemnly, she repeated, "Friends."

"Then as your friend, I have to tell you that there's an inchworm dangling about yea high over your head, ready to make a landing. Shall I divert him to another landing field?"

"If you would be so kind." She sighed, rolled her eyes and said, "I think I might be the teeniest bit sozzled. I'm not used to all this wild living and champagne drinking and—and everything."

He was silent for a full minute, then he said, "I think it might be a good idea if I got you home. I'd suggest a shower and an early night." So much for the fancy dinner.

"Not a shower, a soak. A nice, deep soak, with no one knocking on the bathroom door telling me to hurry up, and not to use all the hot water." Her face fell. "I guess Maura will be home from shopping by now, though. She'll have things that need doing."

"For once she can do them herself." Hitch wanted to tell her to quit being a damned doormat. He wanted to tell her to stand up against petty tyranny, to develop some backbone, but it wasn't his place to tell her anything.

Watching her come up on her knees, lean down on one elbow, butt in the air, and carefully replace the disposable flutes in the picnic basket, he knew what it was he really wanted, and it scared the hell out of him.

He wanted to keep her.

"Hitch, could I ask a favor?" Mama Mac, wearing a fresh apron over what she called a housedress, placed a stack of pancakes on his plate. "You know all that junk Aldous has stored in the garage? I told him if he didn't straighten it out I was going to call Goodwill to come haul it off."

"You want me to clean up your garage?"

She patted him on the shoulder. "Lawsy no, honey, I want you to tell him how to organize his storage, the way you did when Mac had to go through all the stuff at that first ski place of his. You're good at organizing. Aldous couldn't organize a plate of bacon and eggs. He'd just pile one thing on top of the other with the toast on the bottom."

That pretty well shot Hitch's plan to get out of temptation's way. Working outside, with the Stephensons' place just on the other side of the hedge, he was bound to see her.

And if he saw her, he could hardly ignore her. They'd say hello, and next thing he knew they'd be talking about the kinds of things he never talked about with anyone, and he'd be thinking things he had no business thinking.

At least, not about Cindy Danbury.

On the other hand, he might just do her one last favor.

The idea took root and started to grow when Pop mentioned a kid he'd coached a few years ago who was playing triple-A baseball. "Name of Pete Simmons. Fine boy. Girls were all crazy about him, but he didn't let it get in the way of what he wanted, nosiree. Still single, last I heard. Coulda' made it in football, too—kinda wish he had, but hey, an athlete's an athlete, and Pete's going to make a name for himself in the majors one of these days."

Pete, as it happened, was home for a few days, and had called to say he'd be by to see Pop this morning.

Why not? Hitch asked himself. Sure, she hated matchmaking. They both did. But there was nothing wrong with exposing her to a decent guy and letting nature take its course.

Up to a point, he amended with a frown.

And if that didn't work out, there was always Joe Digby. He'd enjoyed seeing good ol' Joe again at the party. The guy had earned himself a degree in electrical engineering, but had ended up with his own landscaping business, specializing in roses. Cindy would like a man who could talk flowers with her. Introducing her to a couple of fellows he happened to know wasn't exactly matchmaking. Was it?

And even if it was, she'd be a damned sight better

off finding a nice guy to marry than moving out on her own and trying to make a career out of designing hats.

Did women even wear hats these days?

Hitch thought later that he couldn't have planned it better if he'd done it deliberately. Maura was out every night, and as Cindy was all alone, Mama Mac invited her to supper the same night Pop invited his protégé, the triple-A pitcher.

Hitch felt like a benign godfather. He sat back and watched as Cindy, who knew little about sports, listened with every appearance of being fascinated while Pete talked about his hopes of being called up to the majors now that two of the big league pitchers were out on DL.

"What's DL?" she asked, tackling her plate of Mama Mac's roast pork and sweet potatoes. Hitch had to wonder where she put it, because she couldn't weigh more than a hundred pounds soaking wet.

Expanding under her genuine interest, Pete explained about the many afflictions ball players suffered, and how some of them went on the disabled list for an entire season. Before he drove off, they'd made a date to go into Winston to see a movie the following night.

After Pete left, Cindy, who'd insisted on helping with the dishes, said, "I probably should've checked with Maura first to see what her plans are."

"Does she check with you about yours?" Hitch inquired.

"Well, no…but then, I never have plans, except on Mondays."

"Go. I'll square it with Maura, if it comes to that."

So she went. Hitch was watching from next door when Pete picked her up the following evening. He drove a brand-new red pickup bristling with chrome accessories. It was high. Cindy was not. Pete had to lift her up into the passenger seat, and Hitch, watching through the window, felt his fists curling at his side.

"She's not your young'un, Son," Pop said, laying aside the *Winston-Salem Journal*.

"No, but she's a good friend. I'd hate to see anyone take advantage of her inexperience."

Pop raised his eyebrows, but went back to the sports page without further comment.

It was after eleven when Hitch heard the muffled growl of Pete's truck pull up outside the house next door. Rising, he stretched and sauntered over to the front door. "Think I'll step outside for a breath of fresh air before I turn in," he remarked, and Pop grinned, but didn't turn away from the TV.

Hitch waited until her date drove off, and then he rapped on the front door. She opened it almost immediately. She was barefooted, holding her shoes in her hand.

"Well?" he asked.

"Well, what?"

"How'd it go?"

"Better than my last date, at least."

"That good, huh?"

"We mostly talked about league standings and all the things that can go wrong with a pitcher's arm, and how umpires are blind, and managers don't always know everything.''

"And you'd rather talk about hats?''

"No—well, yes, I guess I would, but we could've talked about a few other things.''

"He was probably trying to impress you.''

"Impress *me?* My mercy, why would he want to do that?''

Hitch sighed. He was tempted to tell her. With any other woman, he'd have thought she was fishing for compliments, but Cindy wasn't like any other woman. She was…

Yeah, well. "Better say good-night. I've got a day's work ahead of me tomorrow. We're building shelves across the back of the garage.''

"Pop Mac's a good carpenter. I guess he just never thought about building shelves out there. Sometimes it's hard to see what's in front of your very nose.''

Hitch leaned closer. They were standing on the front porch in plain view of anyone who happened to be passing by, so he figured he wouldn't be taking too great a risk in giving in to an impulse.

"Let's see what's in front of your nose,'' he said, his voice soft on account of the late hour.

She lifted her face just as if she knew what was coming, and he leaned closer. Their lips met. Resisting the urge to taste her, he drew away and gazed at her nose. "There, I thought that's what the trouble was.''

"What trouble?''

"He forgot to kiss you, didn't he?''

"Well, no…I mean, I don't think he wanted to.

We just watched the movie and got ice cream cones, and then we talked all the way home. He's really nice, Hitch, but if you're trying to start something, I'd better tell you he's got a girl in Durham.''

"Scratch one hot prospect from the list."

"I should have realized—I didn't think until I'd already said yes, but you deliberately set this up, didn't you?"

"Maybe—yeah, I guess I did, but only because I want you to know you have options.''

Slowly, she shook her head. She was wearing something yellow and summery, and looked years younger than the twenty-four and a half he knew her to be.

"I appreciate it, Hitch, I really do, but you know how I feel about matchmaking. It never works out.''

"Never?"

"Almost never. Never in my case, anyway, because I've got my future all mapped out, and men don't figure in it anywhere. I won't have time for years and years.''

A car drove past slowly. Through the open window of the house next door, the hall clock began its midnight count, which meant Pop had already switched off the TV and headed upstairs.

Which meant that Hitch had better cut this short.

He kissed her again, because he couldn't put into words what he wanted to say.

Wouldn't have said it, even if he could have found the words.

Chapter Five

Hitch didn't try to kid himself any longer. What he was up to was matchmaking, pure and simple. Something he and Cindy both despised. Worse still was his reason for doing it.

Self-protection.

This time it wasn't quite so easy to talk her into it. She was wary, but he was counting on the fact that she was a soft touch.

"I first met Joe the same time I met Mac, in our freshman year at Tech. Mac and I sort of adopted him, you might say. Poor kid was painfully shy, never had developed much in the way of social skills. Too busy, I guess. He worked his way through college, and Mac says he took care of his mother after his father died. Then, when she passed away a few years ago, he carried on the family business. As I said, he's a great guy."

"I'm sure he is," Cindy said evenly, "but you know how I feel about blind dates."

"Yeah. Joe feels the same way. We used to try to fix him up back in Atlanta, but it never worked out. At least you've got that much in common." Hitch gave her what he hoped was a disarming smile. "Joe was going to take his cousin to his high school reunion tomorrow night, but something came up and she can't make it. Without a date, he won't go, and you know what they say about all work and no play.... Joe really needs a break."

In the end, Cindy reluctantly agreed to go to the reunion with Joe Digby, landscape gardener and old college classmate, as a special favor to Hitch. When Hitch introduced them, Joe said he sort of remembered her from when he used to drop by Mac's house.

Cindy said she sort of remembered him, too, from living next door to Mac. Hitch didn't know if it was true or if she was just trying to put his friend at ease. Joe Digby wasn't what you'd call a memorable fellow. Bald as an egg, he had the guileless eyes of a child and a smile that could melt granite. He was thoroughly decent, though. Cindy would come to no harm.

And if she enjoyed the evening, who knew where it could lead?

After they drove off together in Joe's van, Hitch wandered back through the hedge. The smug expression on his face gave way to a thoughtful look, and then a frown.

"Come have some blackberry cobbler, Hitch," Mama Mac called. "I just took it out of the oven. Wash up first."

They ate cobbler drowned in homemade custard

sauce, and talked, watched the evening news and talked some more, mostly about Mac and Steff. After the elder Macs turned in, Hitch wandered out onto the front porch again and glanced over the hedge to the house next door. Unless Joe had changed over the past ten years or so, they'd be rolling up most anytime now. Joe was an early to bed, early to rise type.

"What in the world are you doing here? You startled me, popping out of the shadows that way!"

Hitch had strolled over to the Stephensons' place and settled in the swing, which was all the way at the end of the porch, shaded from the streetlight by a swag of wisteria. At the last minute, watching Joe hold her carefully by the arm as he walked her to the front door, Hitch wished he'd simply gone to bed, but by then it was too late to escape undetected.

He rose nobly to the occasion. "I figured Maura wouldn't wait up, and I thought someone should check to be sure you got home okay."

"I'm an adult, Hitch. I don't need a baby-sitter."

"I'm not—well, sure you are, that's not the point."

She waited with exaggerated patience for him to say good-night and leave. The humidity, or something, had done a number on her hair. With the yellow bug light behind her, she looked as if she were wearing a halo.

He cleared his throat and hauled his brain back in line. "The thing is, I sort of feel responsible. I mean, I was the one to introduce you to Joe. So...how'd the reunion go?"

Cindy slipped off her shoes and dangled them by the straps from one finger. "We had a marvelous time! I knew at least half the people there. Hitch, did you know moles are a protected species?"

He did a fast mental double take. "Moles? Oh— you mean the animal kind of moles. Uh...no, I didn't."

"Joe has the most fascinating store of information. He said there's a plant called—I forget what he called it, it's one of those latin names, but it's supposed to keep moles away because it's against the law to poison them, only—"

"Cindy."

"—it multiplies so fast it fills up your garden, so—"

"Cindy."

"What?" She shifted her weight onto the other hip and raked her hair behind her ears with her free hand. It was hard to tell in the artificial light, but he thought her face looked flushed. In fact, she looked as if she'd had a great time.

Too great a time. "Did you dance?"

"Some, but mostly, we talked. Joe's not real comfortable on the dance floor. I think he's shy."

"I told you he was shy, remember?" It was the only reason she'd gone out with him; Hitch was convinced of that. "You look pretty tonight, by the way." She was wearing the yellow again. It was the only thing he'd seen her wear that looked as if she'd picked it out and tried it on first. Even her jeans were too loose.

"Thank you. And thank you for waiting up. No one's ever done that before." Then, with that quirky smile that started in her eyes, creased one cheek and moved to her lips, she added, "Of course, I'm usually in long before bedtime."

She didn't seem particularly eager to escape. He took that as a good sign. He could have watched from the porch next door to see that she got in safely, but he'd thought maybe a debriefing was in order. Just in case anything had come up that she needed to talk over with a disinterested party.

Hell, he'd have done the same thing for a little sister if he'd been lucky enough to have one.

"Didn't Joe forget something?"

She settled into the swing beside Hitch and set it in motion with one foot. "I don't think so." She tilted her head, a puzzled frown on her face.

"I didn't see him kiss you good-night."

She planted both feet on the floor, causing the swing to jerk back and forth. "Well, my mercy, it was only our first date. What did you expect?"

He shrugged. "These days you never know. Does that mean you're going out with him again?"

She set the swing to moving again. "I might. If he asks me. He probably won't."

"Why the devil not? What did you say to discourage him?"

She laughed. "Hitch, in case you hadn't noticed, I'm hardly the kind of woman men trip all over themselves to go out with."

"What's wrong with you? Scratch that, what I meant was—"

"For one thing, I'm not pretty." When he would have interrupted, she went on to say, "And I'm too outspoken. Men don't like a woman who speaks her mind.''

"Since when did you turn into an expert on what men like?''

"Since growing up around Steff and Maura. I might not have had all that much personal experience, but I've certainly heard all about theirs.''

"I'm glad you didn't say hands-on experience.'' It was a snide comment. Other than jabbing him in the side with her elbow, Cindy ignored it.

"For instance, I know men like beautiful women who flatter them and make them feel intelligent whether they are or not, and they like—'' She broke off and twisted her fingers in her lap.

Hitch stilled her hands with his. "They like what?'' he prompted.

"You know.''

"Yeah, I probably do, but since you claim to be the expert, why don't you tell me?''

"I didn't claim to be an expert, and I don't have to tell you everything I know.''

"I thought you were so outspoken. Cindy? Is it sex you can't bring yourself to talk about?''

"Oh, for heaven's sake, it's practically the middle of the night. Do we have to do this? Can the inquisition wait until tomorrow?''

"It can wait forever,'' he said quietly. He shifted slightly, dropped his arm from the back of the swing to her shoulder. Inhaling the light, sweet scent that was hers and hers alone, he said, "I don't think this can wait, though.''

With one hand, he tipped her face up to his. It was an awkward position—he didn't know how front porch swings had come to be so highly regarded for this sort of activity, but he was here, and she was here, and he wasn't about to rock the boat, so to speak, by suggesting they go inside.

Light from the yellow bulb beside the front door drained the fiery color from her hair, lent an exotic cast to her delicate features. Her blue eyes were shadowy pools of mystery. He hesitated only briefly before lowering his lips to hers.

She stiffened, but then melted almost immediately. Her mouth was even sweeter than he'd remembered. Incredibly soft, warm and slightly moist. Nudging guilt aside, he took shameless advantage of her obvious inexperience.

She's young, he told himself, but not *too* young. Naive, but not totally without experience. What girl over fifteen in this day and age was?

All the same, he made a conscious effort not to allow things to get out of hand. One simple kiss, he promised himself, then he'd say good-night and leave.

Trouble was, it was no simple kiss. He was beginning to believe nothing was simple where this woman was concerned. When he eventually lifted his face to gaze down at her, her eyes were closed. They remained that way for several seconds, and then she sighed and fluttered them open.

"That was nice," she whispered, smiling up at him.

"Nice?"

Nice? Did she have any idea at all what she was doing to him? Physically as well as mentally?

"But Hitch, you aren't obligated to kiss me good-night after every date. Just because you introduced me to Pete and Joe, that doesn't mean you're responsible for—''

He started to swear and stopped just in time. ''Listen to me, Cindy, I did not kiss you out of any sense of obligation.''

''You didn't? Then why?''

''Why? Because I— Because you— How the devil do I know why I did it? Because you were there, and I was here, and I wanted this evening to be special for you.''

''Obligation. That's what I thought.'' Still smiling, she said quietly, ''It *was* special, all right? Friends?''

He gave up. Flat out surrendered. ''Friends,'' he echoed, defeated. Rising, he muttered something about seeing her tomorrow, and left before he got in any deeper.

Left before he did something irreparably stupid.

Before he did something *else* irreparably stupid.

''I think I'd better be getting back to Richmond today,'' he told the woman who was ladling grits onto his plate from the blue enamel pot on the stove.

''Today? Why, you only just got here. I thought you were going to stay at least a week.''

''Yeah, I thought so, too, but the longer I stay away, the deeper the pile on my desk when I get back. When it gets to be more than a foot high, I sweep it into the trash and start over. Lose a lot of business that way.''

''Oh, go on with you, you'd never do that,'' Mama Mac chided. She slapped a pat of butter on his grits and slid the platter of bacon and eggs closer.

Hitch spent the rest of the morning helping put up the last shelf across the back wall of the garage. It was the least he could do before he left. The Macs were more like family than his own parents had ever been. He'd have to make it a point not to stay away so long.

On the other hand, maybe he'd invite them to Richmond. It might be safer, at least until things changed next door.

He started to pack his bag, but discovered that half his shirts were on the line drying. "I'll iron them for you as soon as they're dry," Mama Mac promised.

"You don't have to do that," he told her, but she waved him away as if he were a little boy being sent out into the backyard to play.

Which meant he had plenty of time to go next door and say goodbye to Cindy. It meant running the risk of seeing Maura again, but he could handle that easily. He'd been handling it ever since he'd arrived, when Mac had warned him to watch out because she'd lined him up in the crosshairs. That might have been true once, but she seemed to have lost interest.

What he wasn't at all sure he could handle was seeing Cindy one more time. Practically running her down in the street that first day had been bad enough, but they'd gotten beyond that. Oh, yeah, they'd done that, all right. If he ran off now, he'd end up feeling like dirt all over again. He might be a coward, but he did have principles.

* * *

Cindy tugged her gardening gloves over hands that were slick with lotion. She'd started using the industrial strength stuff ever since Hitch had kissed her calluses. She'd been so embarrassed she could have sunk through the floor. What good were satin gowns and high-heel shoes when her hands looked as if they belonged to a mechanic?

She'd come outside to pull up the scraggly tomato vines and get the ground ready for the collard slips. Aunt S. allowed her only a tiny plot for vegetables and flowers together; she had to make the most of every inch.

"Cindy?"

Slapping a gloved hand to her breast, she spun around so fast she nearly fell. "You scared the wits out of me, sneaking up like that!"

It was Hitch. He stopped and stared at her as if she'd lost her mind, which she probably had as she'd barely been able to sleep a wink for thinking about him. Wondering when he would be leaving, knowing that once he left, she'd probably never see him again. Mac and Steff would be living at one of Mac's ski lodges, so Hitch would have no real reason to come back to Mocksville.

"Want me to back off and try again? How about if I whistle this time?"

"What I want is—"

What I want is you, she was tempted to tell him. That would scare him off in a hurry. Darn it, he had no business kissing her when it meant less than nothing to him and everything to her. No doubt he was used to kissing, but she wasn't.

Once, a long time ago, she'd stepped through the hedge to return a cake tin to Mama Mac and caught sight of a tall, good-looking guy kissing a girl—nuzzling her, lifting his head to gaze down at her with lazy, hungry-looking eyes. Cindy couldn't have been more than fifteen years old then. Old enough to fall in love, but not old enough to do anything about it.

Over the years he had come to be a regular guest next door, and she had watched from afar. Watched and dreamed, and listened to Steff and Maura whisper excitedly about a man called Hitch, who was "way cool" and "laid-back" and so sexy someone named MayDale had actually hidden in his room, stark naked, and waited for him to come to bed, only Mama Mac had gone upstairs to put extra blankets in all the guest rooms, and that had been the end of that.

"I guess you came to say goodbye," Cindy said. "I thought you'd probably be leaving today." She started to remove her grimy gloves, thought about her ragged nails and rough skin and left them on.

"I guess you're right," he said laconically. Still laid-back. Still way cool. Still sexier than the law allowed.

"Well...goodbye, then," she said, and forced what she hoped was a convincing smile.

"Got a headache? Too much partying last night?"

"Mercy, why would you think that? I feel terrific!"

"Something's wrong. Is there anything I can do?"

"I need to get my collard slips in before the weather changes. They're calling for rain starting tonight and lasting for the next few days. Something about a tropical depression along the coast."

"Listen, you don't have to do this, you know."

She looked around at the scrawny bean vines, surrounded by marigolds and nasturtiums that were supposed to keep the bugs away, but didn't. At the worn-out okra that had been so lovely only a few weeks earlier, with its yellow, hibiscuslike blossoms. At the bundle of collard slips, wrapped in wet newspapers, that she intended to plant, even if she was no longer here to see them mature.

Then she looked at the man who had come to tell her he was leaving. "Yes, I do," she said gruffly.

He moved closer, gripped her shoulders and turned her to face him. It was all she could do not to burst out bawling like a five-year-old who'd just learned the truth about the tooth fairy. She sniffed and caught the enticing aroma of shaving soap and sun-dried linens.

"Have you ever thought about taking a course at the community college? Most of them have night classes."

"They teach hat design?"

He shook her. Ever so gently, but she could tell he didn't have a whole lot of patience with her life-long ambition. "They teach practical things like—well, maybe real estate. Or computer programming—something marketable."

"What if someone had advised Rembrandt, or Renoir, or Monet to go into real estate or computer progamming? Hitch, I know you mean well, but I have faith in me, even if you don't.''

He reached out to her again, but this time his hand fell short. ''I do. That's just the trouble, Cindy—I have a lot of faith in you. What I don't have much faith in is the buying public. They might not be, uh—ready for what you have to offer.''

''You have no idea what I have to offer. Wait here,'' she said, and suddenly spun away, leaving him standing there between the pole bean stakes and the bare okra stalks. ''Don't you dare go away!'' she called over her shoulder as she disappeared into the house.

Well, hell, Hitch thought. He'd brought it on himself by coming over here in the first place. Should've known nothing was simple where Cindy was concerned. He had known it, in fact. Last night, if not sooner.

But before he could slink through the hedge to safety, she was back, carrying a stack of boxes higher than her head. ''Take these things,'' she panted. ''Careful! Just set them down over there.'' From behind the stack, she nodded to the back steps.

When he did as she asked, she dusted off her hands and then opened a box, lifting out what appeared to be a jumble of flowers. Wearing baggy jeans and a T-shirt that had seen better days, she planted the thing on her head, put on her grubby gardening gloves again and struck a pose.

''These are just working models, you understand. I can't afford high quality materials, but the design is what counts, and I can't get a feel for the design with only sketches. I call this one Belle,'' she said airily. "I give all my hats women's names. One of these days I'll have my own name on a satin ribbon in the back of each one. Cindy. Or maybe Cynthia, I haven't decided yet."

Before he could think of a single thing to say, she set Belle carefully back in its box and tried on another creation, this one yellow straw and paper sunflowers with a butterfly pinning up one side of the brim.

She pranced.

He applauded. He was grinning—not quite laughing, but he felt like laughing. Lord, she was something else!

"Now this one is my favorite, but it's not for everyday. Maybe a wedding or something." Carefully, she settled a concoction of pale pink and ivory roses dotted with pearl dewdrops on top of her wild red hair. "I call it Pearl's Mama."

"Pearl's what?"

"Officially, it's Mother of Pearl, but it's one of my pets, so I gave it a nickname. Don't you just love it?"

"Yeah, I love it," he said softly. Funny thing— he really did. Not that that meant a whole lot, because what he knew about women's fashions amounted to what he liked and what he didn't like.

What he didn't like was the kind of clothes his mother's colleagues wore. The man-tailored suits and clunky shoes. They might be fine in a law office, but they didn't do a damned thing for him as a man.

Right now he liked what Cindy was wearing, which proved he had totally lost it. Baggy jeans, a sagging T-shirt and muddy gloves. Even her sneakers had a hole in one toe. Either those hats of hers were magic or he was in even deeper trouble than he'd suspected.

"There now, are you convinced? Just one more, and I'll—" She was prancing past him, lifting both hands to remove Pearl's Mama, when she tripped on her shoestring. Grabbing the hat, she would have fallen if Hitch hadn't managed to catch her. "Whoa, watch your step," he cautioned.

"Oh, my," she said breathlessly, still clutching her hat.

There was no way on earth he could help himself, not with her gazing up at him, eyes wide, lips parted, grimy canvas gloves hanging on to that ridiculous, pearl-bedewed confection of a hat.

So he kissed her. Having sworn not to make the same mistake again, he made it. In broad daylight.

Holding her hat with one hand, she slid the other hand to his neck, then raked her gloved fingers through his hair. Her lips parted like a flower opening to the sun. She tasted of coffee and honey, and her own unique sweetness.

Savoring the moment, Hitch shamelessly took advantage of it and might have taken even more had not a door slammed close by. They broke apart, both breathless, both slightly dazed.

Maura, wearing a brief, kelly-green knit dress, her streaked hair flawlessly groomed, stood glaring at them from the side porch. Her face was mottled with angry color.

Oh, hell.

Closing his eyes briefly, Hitch wished he'd had the good sense to get out of town while the getting was good. Mac had warned him. Unfortunately, he'd warned him about the wrong woman, but it was too late now.

"Where are they?" Maura demanded.

"Who?" Hitch asked before he realized the question was directed at Cindy, not him. The look Maura sent him said, "Butt out, I'll take care of you later."

At least that was the way he interpreted it.

Cindy looked flustered. She smiled, but it wasn't a wholly successful effort. "They're probably playing golf—I'm not sure about the time diff—"

"Where the hell are my earrings?"

"Your earrings?"

Her earrings? Hitch stared at the irate woman on the porch.

"You heard me! My best pearl-and-diamond earrings, the ones I lent you for the rehearsal party— against my better judgment, I might add!"

"Oh, but I—"

"I took everything out of my jewelry case, and they're not there. You were the last one to wear them, so—"

"But I didn't wear them, I put them on your dresser. Your case is always locked, and anyway, I'd never have opened it."

"Hey, hold on, now," Hitch said.

Both women ignored him. "I've searched everything in your bedroom except that junk you've got there, so if you've hidden them in with those wretched hats of yours, you might as well hand them over, otherwise I'm reporting it."

Of the three, Cindy remained calmest. Her face had paled until the only color that remained was her freckles and her blue eyes. Both stood out in stark contrast. Hitch didn't know which to do first—hide her in his arms, hat and all, or shake Maura until her back teeth rattled.

"There's obviously been some kind of a mistake," he said in his most placating tone.

Both women turned on him. Maura said, "This doesn't concern you—it's between me and this little thief!"

Cindy said quietly, "Let it be, Hitch, they probably fell down behind the dresser. I'll find them. And if I don't see you before you leave, have a happy…" Her lips trembled. She turned and hurried inside the house, still holding Pearl's Mama, leaving the rest of her precious hats scattered along the edge of the porch.

Chapter Six

Casting one anguished glance over her shoulder, Cindy followed Maura up the stairs. It was all a misunderstanding—of course it was—but Maura didn't have to be quite so spiteful. It was embarrassing. The worst thing about it was Hitch's leaving with this parting impression of her.

No, the worst thing was his leaving at all.

Pausing to catch her breath on the top step, she followed her into the bedroom, which looked even worse than usual because Maura was in the process of moving into Steff's old bedroom and packing to go to New York at the same time. It didn't make much sense to Cindy, but then, she knew better than to question anything a Stephenson did. Maura had always been possessive, both with people and things.

"I put them right here." Cindy pointed at a place on the dresser between a mirrored tray of perfumes, a large, locked jewelry case and a silver-backed hairbrush. The rest of the dresser clutter had been raked off into a box, ready to be either packed or carried into the corner room.

"Sure you did," Maura said sarcastically. "So where are they?"

"Maybe they got caught up in some of the things you've packed."

"Get real. I know what I've packed."

"Then they probably just slipped down behind the dresser."

"They're not there. I looked."

"Maura, I distinctly remember—"

"Remember what, pawning them? I hope you got your money's worth, because diamonds and pearls don't come cheap."

"I would never—"

"Then where are they? I searched everything in your room except those awful hats of yours." She stared pointedly at the confection Cindy still held, of palest silk and velvet roses with tiny faux pearls sewn carefully on a few petals. "Oh, God, I bet you decorated one of your tacky hats with my best earrings! It would be just like you!"

Cindy felt about two inches high. "You know I'd never do anything like that," she whispered, more hurt than angry. They'd been family for so long now. Like most families, they had their differences, but Maura and Steff and Aunt S. were all she had left.

"Then tell me where they are, and don't expect me to believe they both happened to fall off your ears at the same time and get lost."

"They were never—"

"I should've had better sense, but when you went whining to Hitch, and he told Mama, and she made Steff lend you that gown and those matching shoes, Steff said I had to do my part. I should've—"

Ignoring all the rest, Cindy said, "Maura, they couldn't have fallen from my ears because I never even wore them. My ears aren't pierced—I thought you knew that." Cindy felt sure she had known it, but it wouldn't help to argue the point now. "I'm sorry. I'll do everything I can to find them, but—"

"We should never have let Daddy talk us into taking you into our home in the first place. You're not even a real Danbury. Mama says your mother was no better than she should be!"

"Maura, if I can't find them, I'll pay whatever they cost." There was a sound in her ears like rushing water, and she knew if she didn't get out of that room quickly she would say something awful and spend the rest of her life regretting it.

"Pay me back? Ha! With what, may I ask?" Maura jeered, her face mottled with color. "Don't tell me you're finally going to sell that old clunker of yours? You can't even afford to have it hauled off to the junkyard, much less repaired."

Cindy's car was one more bone of contention. All three of the Stephenson women were embarrassed to have a secondhand subcompact that had not aged particularly well parked outside their three-car garage, but there was no room inside. And junky or not, Uncle Henry had given it to her and so they couldn't say too much. He'd given both Steff and

Maura cars on their eighteenth birthdays, too—theirs new, of course.

"It just needs a new alternator," she explained quietly. "Once I get it running again I'm planning to have it painted."

"Either you give me back my earrings or I'm calling the junkyard to come get it. There are zoning laws against abandoned cars, and Mama's best friend's husband is a county commissioner."

Cindy had a quick temper. One quick blast and it was over.

Maura had a truly vicious temper. It hung on and on like a bad summer cold, making everyone within range of her tantrums miserable. Head held high, Cindy did the only thing left to do. She clamped her lips together and walked out.

Pausing outside the door to catch her breath, she tried hard to visualize placing the earrings on Maura's dresser. She distinctly remembered wishing she could lock them away, not that she'd thought for a single minute anyone would bother them. People simply didn't do that sort of thing, not in this neighborhood. Not in this household.

Could Steff have borrowed them for her honeymoon?

Hardly likely. Steff had tons of jewelry of her own. Danbury heirlooms, gifts from an indulgent father, even a few pieces she'd bought herself. To Steff's way of thinking, a twenty-percent-off sale was reason enough to buy anything, if only because it gave her a perfect excuse to go back and spend the money she claimed to have saved.

Cindy wished now she hadn't eaten those waffles

for breakfast. Her stomach was churning and her head was starting to throb. And she'd thought once they got through the wedding, her troubles would be over.

Charlie. He'd been into everything. Could he have...?

No, not Charlie. He'd been under someone's eagle eye from the first day. If not her own, then his mother's. Charlie was a menace, but he wasn't a thief.

So...either the blasted things had walked off or one of the bridesmaids had borrowed them and forgotten to return them, neither of which was likely. No one else had been upstairs, so far as Cindy knew. She cleaned the rooms herself, changing the linen, vacuuming, dusting, gathering up whatever needed washing or dry-cleaning. There was simply no other possibility. The blasted things *had* to be somewhere in this house!

Standing in the middle of the second floor hall, eyes shut tight, she whispered, "If I were a pair of earrings, where would I be?"

She was still trying to come up with an answer when Maura's door swung open. "I'll give you one hour to remember where you hid my earrings, and then I'm calling the sheriff."

Even with work piling up in his absence and an early morning appointment in Richmond, Hitch hated like the very devil to leave. The missing earrings would turn up, he had no doubt of that, but dammit, it made him furious to see Cindy humiliated that way.

Here's a **HOT** offer for you!

Get set for a sizzling summer read...

with **2 FREE ROMANCE BOOKS**
and a **FREE MYSTERY GIFT!**
NO CATCH! NO OBLIGATION TO BUY!

Simply complete and return this card and you'll get **2 FREE BOOKS** and **A FREE GIFT** – yours to keep!

Visit us online at www.eHarlequin.com

🌀 The first shipment is yours to keep, **absolutely free!**

🌀 Enjoy the convenience of Silhouette Romance® books delivered right to your door, before they're available in stores!

🌀 Take advantage of special low pricing for **Reader Service Members only!**

🌀 After receiving your free books we hope you'll want to remain a subscriber. But the choice is always yours—to continue or cancel, any time at all! So why not take us up on this fabulous invitation, with no risk of any kind. You'll be glad you did!

315 SDL C26P

215 SDL C26K
(S-R-OS-06/00)

Name:	
(Please Print)	
Address:	Apt.#:
City:	
State/Prov.:	Zip/ Postal Code:

◄ DETACH HERE AND MAIL CARD TODAY! ▼

The Silhouette Reader Service™ —Here's how it works:

Accepting your 2 free books and gift places you under no obligation to buy anything. You may keep the books and gift and return the shipping statement marked "cancel." If you do not cancel, about a month later we'll send you 6 additional novels and bill you just $2.90 each in the U.S., or $3.25 each in Canada, plus 25¢ delivery per book and applicable taxes if any.* That's the complete price and — compared to cover prices of $3.50 each in the U.S. and $3.99 each in Canada — it's quite a bargain! You may cancel at any time, but if you choose to continue, every month we'll send you 6 more books, which you may either purchase at the discount price or return to us and cancel your subscription.

*Terms and prices subject to change without notice. Sales tax applicable in N.Y. Canadian residents will be charged applicable provincial taxes and GST.

If offer card is missing write to: Silhouette Reader Service, 3010 Walden Ave., P.O. Box 1867, Buffalo, NY 14240-1867

NO POSTAGE
NECESSARY
IF MAILED
IN THE
UNITED STATES

BUSINESS REPLY MAIL
FIRST-CLASS MAIL   PERMIT NO. 717   BUFFALO, NY

POSTAGE WILL BE PAID BY ADDRESSEE

SILHOUETTE READER SERVICE
3010 WALDEN AVE
PO BOX 1867
BUFFALO NY   14240-9952

Maura had probably mislaid the things herself, not that she'd ever admit it, much less apologize. It would fall to Cindy to patch things up, smooth them over so the two women—three when the dragon lady returned—could go on sharing a roof until Maura headed north.

He bagged his tux, zipped it shut and slung it across the foot of the bed, his mind still on the scene next door. Lord, she'd looked enchanting wearing those absurd hats, with her ratty garden gloves and her cute little fanny shaping the seat of those baggy jeans. He tried and failed to picture any of the women he'd gone out with over the past few years pulling a stunt like that.

Funny, the way you could get to know someone in the space of only a few days. He'd known Maura for years—at least as well as he cared to know her. She'd sent out plenty of signals, but a deep-seated sense of self-preservation had kept him from responding.

He'd known Cindy for little more than a week. In that short time he'd come to know her courage, her innate honesty. He knew that no matter how pushed she was, how hard she worked, laughter came easily to her. She sang and often whistled when she worked, which he happened to know drove Mrs. S. crazy.

Might even be the reason she did it, he thought, amused. She had spunk, for all her lack of size. If her dreams were, in his estimation, highly impractical, they were her dreams, not his. She was entitled to them.

His own parents had never understood why he

had marched to his own drummer rather than follow the family calling. He'd like to believe he was a big enough man not to rain on Cindy's parade just because he didn't happen to share her vision.

After packing and loading his car, including enough fried chicken, pickled okra and German chocolate cake to last him for a week, he went back inside to say his goodbyes. He hugged Mama Mac, kissed her on a plump, vanilla-scented cheek, shook Pop's hand and then embraced him, too.

"No, don't come outside, it's sweltering hot, probably going to cut loose with a thunderstorm any minute now," Hitch exclaimed. As if in response, thunder rumbled ominously. "Pop, think about that overhead storage we talked about. It's good space going to waste. Mama—no, don't you start up now, or I'll cry, too, and you don't want that on your conscience."

"Oh, go on, you," she chided, and he grinned.

He wouldn't cry. Hadn't since he was about five—but he knew he was going to miss them both.

Promising not to allow so much time to pass between visits, he decided to make a point of dropping in once or twice a year. The MacCollums weren't getting any younger, and Mac was going to have his hands full with Steff from now on.

Hitch was thinking about all that, not really concentrating, as he strode out into the looming storm to hear Maura's shrill voice coming from the other side of the hedge.

"The only reason I'm letting you go and not calling the sheriff is because I won't have you dragging the Danbury name through the mud!"

What the devil?

He dumped his bags and pushed through the time-worn gap in the hedge. Cindy was—what, taking out the garbage? Through the front door?

"Everybody knows you're not even a real Danbury!" Maura yelled after her. "Everybody knows we took you in when we didn't have to, and this is the thanks we get!"

Just as the first fat drops began to fall, Cindy turned, shifted one of the huge plastic bags she was carrying and said calmly, "Maura? Shut. Up."

Hitch's jaw dropped. So far, neither woman had noticed him. He didn't know what the hell was going on, but he did know one thing. He could no more walk away now than he could flap his arms and fly. Cindy had a temper, all right, but that wasn't temper he'd heard, it was quiet desperation. It was rope's end.

He was halfway across the yard, skirting the big magnolia, when Maura slammed the front door, rattling the stained glass panels in their leaded frames.

"Problem?"

Cindy turned just as he reached her side. Her eyes were drenched—maybe it was the rain, he thought, knowing it wasn't. She blinked and managed an unconvincing smile that hinted she was emotionally in way over her head.

"Can I help you with your—uh, with that?" He nodded to the two leaf-and-lawn-size trash bags she'd been dragging. Her empty hat boxes were blowing across the tattered garden.

"You could call me a taxi. I don't know the number."

"Never mind that, where are you going?"

"Anywhere. Winston. Or maybe Charlotte, I haven't decided."

"By taxi?" He wondered if she knew how much it would cost. She'd mentioned having a savings account, but a cab ride to Charlotte was going to put a dent in it. "Why don't I drive you wherever you want to go?" Mentally, he reshuffled his schedule. "We can talk on the way."

She protested politely, then crumbled in a way that made him want to sweep her up and take her home with him, make her hot cocoa and tell her everything was going to be all right.

Only no one had ever done that for him, and he knew better than to try and do it for her.

"There's the bus stop," she said in a small voice. "I can't tell you how to get there, but I can show you."

Mocksville was a small town. A really small town. "When's the next scheduled bus?"

"I don't know," she said simply. He'd buckled her in and tossed her bags in the back seat on top of his tux.

"Know where it's headed?"

"Not really. Away."

Away. That told him something. "Can you afford a ticket to away?"

She looked at him then, all big, bruised eyes and delicate, wobbling chin. "I'm not sure. I think so."

He drove to the center of town and pulled over by the courthouse, under the shelter of an enormous oak. Rain came down in light, gusty waves. A few people huddled in doorways. The air smelled of wet dust.

"Talk," he said. "If I had some idea of what this was all about, I could be of more assistance."

She held it in for so long he was afraid he was going to have to use his lawyering genes, recessive though they were. But then she broke.

"I'm not a thief, I am not," she declared, as if he'd been in any doubt of her honesty. "I don't know where they are—the earrings I was supposed to wear the night of the party—but I did put them right where I said, on Maura's dresser beside her jewelry case. I knew they were valuable—I'd have put them inside, but her case is always kept locked."

He waited. The wrong word at the wrong time, and she'd clam up again.

"Well. There's nothing more I can do. I certainly can't stay there another minute, not with Maura threatening me with the sheriff."

"Did you think of calling your aunt?"

"No."

"Uh...mind my asking why not?" Knowing the dragon lady, he pretty well knew the answer, but they might as well get it all out on the table while they were at it.

"She wouldn't have believed me, either," she said simply, and Hitch nodded. "I have money. At least, I have enough left for a bus ticket and a room, if I get a job real fast."

Her smile damn near broke his heart. "That much, huh?"

"Well, I did have a respectable savings account, at least by my standards, but I wrote Maura a check to pay for the earrings and gave her an IOU for the balance. She wasn't sure how much they'd cost, but she said I should call and she'd let me know when she finds out.''

Cindy shifted uncomfortably and slid her thumb under the seat belt. Hitch had an idea she might be hurting, her pride even more than her hip, but he didn't want to get off the subject of where she planned to go and how the devil she planned to live.

"Okay, so you're broke, you've—''

"No I'm not. I have sixty-three dollars and a bunch of change. That should certainly buy me a bus ticket to Charlotte, and if it won't, I'll settle for Winston-Salem. I wanted to get farther away, not that anyone is likely to come after me, but—

"Cindy, use your brain.''

"I beg your pardon? What do you think I've been using?''

"Your pride. Whatever fuels that fantasy world you live in.''

It got under her skin; he could see that right away. Maybe that was what he'd intended all along—to get her so riled she'd drop her defenses and use some common sense.

His common sense if she couldn't come up with enough of her own. "Okay, here's what we'll do,'' he said decisively. "First, we're going to get out of here. Once this storm blows over we'll stop and reassess the situation. Over food, preferably. I think better on a full stomach. You with me so far?''

He didn't know if she was going to laugh, curse, cry or what. The way she was looking at him, she might even take a swing at him.

Lightning split the sky, followed almost immediately by a cannonade of thunder. She shivered. He unhooked his own seat belt and then hers and tugged her over against his shoulder. She didn't resist, which was a good sign.

At least he thought it was.

"As I was saying," she said, and paused. "What was I saying?"

"We were about to head north for some steak and lobster and a reassessment of your immediate plans. Seems to me two heads are better than one in a case like this."

"I couldn't eat a thing. Maybe some crackers, which I can get in the bus station if you'll drop me off in Winston."

"Crackers. Right," he muttered. Turning the key, he checked behind him for traffic, then made an illegal U-turn and headed north on 158.

A few miles out of town he turned off onto I-40. Neither of them spoke a word until they were crossing the Yadkin River Bridge. Cindy said, "I think there's a get-off near the bus station. I had to take one of my Monday people there once to meet her grandson, who was coming in from military school in Virginia."

He glanced at her curiously. "Your Monday people are going to miss you."

She sighed. "I know. But they've had time to get used to it. With the wedding and my alternator and all, I haven't been able to do very much."

"Your alternator? Is that like a backup plan?"

That, at least, got a smile from her. A sleepy one, but genuine this time. "My car wouldn't charge. I had to have it jumped the last few times I took it out, but now..."

"But now?"

"Well, I guess Maura will have her way, after all. She threatened to sell it for junk. They all hated my car, but Uncle Henry gave it to me, so they couldn't afford to say too much about it." She yawned again.

"Relax, I'll wake you when we get there."

Hitch didn't specify where "there" was, and Cindy was asleep by the time they drove through Clemmons. He saw no point at all in getting off in Winston-Salem to find the bus station. No way would he leave her there, with her two garbage bags and her sixty-odd bucks.

After a while he switched on the radio and found a station that played the kind of music he thought she might like to wake up to. He needed her in the right frame of mind, because getting her to go along with what he had in mind just might be a hard sell. Seeing a drive-in ahead, he tapped the brakes.

She yawned, stretched, opened her eyes and said, " Are we there yet?"

"Almost."

She straightened up, rubbed the back of her neck, then frowned. "It's pitch dark."

"Yep."

"This isn't Winston-Salem."

"Nope."

"Hitch, where are we?"

"Coming up on Green Bay."

"*Wisconsin?*" Twisting, she grabbed his arm, causing him to veer slightly. Luckily the highway was dry. They'd run out of rain just north of the state line.

"Green Bay, Virginia. Now, if you want some supper, quit interfering with the driver. He needs coffee, and he could do with a couple of orders of fries and whatever goes with it."

"Oh, my mercy," she whispered, but to her credit, she didn't panic. Didn't even ask him where the devil he thought he was taking her.

"Like I said, we'll talk over supper," he assured her. It was all he had to offer at the moment, because he didn't know what he was doing, much less why he was doing it. He only knew that there was some kind of a connection between the two of them. One that had been pulling at him ever since he'd nearly run her down that first day.

Maybe even before that, when she'd been a skinny, big-eyed kid looking on from the sidelines while he and Mac and a few of the guys, plus whatever girls they could round up, tried to out-cool each other at the MacCollum place next door.

Cindy flexed her leg muscles and tried to find a position that didn't cramp her hip so much. She wasn't good at sitting, never had been. She'd rather be on the move.

"This is the strangest thing that's ever happened to me. I think. I'm not being kidnapped, am I? Because nobody's going to pay anything to get me back."

"Remember when we decided we were friends?"

She remembered. It was right after he'd kissed her the first time, or maybe the next. But even before he'd kissed her earlier today in the garden, she'd known very well that friendship didn't begin to describe what she felt for this man. On the other hand, if friendship was all she could have, she would take it and try to be grateful.

Dismayed, she eyed the brightly lit fast-food place and tried to decide which hurt more, her bottom, her bladder or her pride.

Pride took third place. She simply had to go to the bathroom, and walk around awhile to ease her joints, and eating wasn't a bad idea, either, because she hadn't had a bite since breakfast.

To quell her growing panic, she chattered. "My mother told me once that redheads burn calories faster than most people, which was why I could eat sweets and not get fat, and she couldn't. Not that she was fat, but then, she was...."

She tugged at her T-shirt, the same one she'd been wearing all day, and smiled to cover her embarrassment. "I need to wash up first, but would you order me a cheeseburger, some fries and pie if they have it and it looks good?"

"You got it," he told her, and she wanted to burrow up in his warm, growly voice and stay there until things began to make sense again. Tender, that's what he was, she decided as she pushed open the door to the ladies' room. He might not look it with his square jaw and his blade of a nose and those deep-set eyes that could bore right into her center, but he was tender.

And kind. She'd seen it in the way he treated the Macs, with love and respect, as if they were as dear to him as his own family.

He was also so sexy she had to keep reminding

herself they were only friends. However, this was no time to complicate matters with inappropriate urges, so she quickly splashed cold water on her face, dried it with a paper towel and wished she'd thought to change into something nicer before she'd marched out.

"I'm not dressed for high dudgeon," she confessed when she slipped into the booth a few minutes later. There were only a few people in the place. Even the staff looked half-asleep.

"Beg pardon?"

"High dudgeon. You know, that thing people get in when they think the world's turned against them for all the wrong reasons?"

"Aha. *That* dudgeon. Well, as to that, I did some thinking while you were dozing and I came up with an idea. Couple of ideas, actually. Want to hear 'em?"

"What are friends for but to listen to each other's ideas?"

He gave her a wry look. "Okay, idea number one is that this thing happened for a reason. You needed something to pry you out of a situation that was stifling your, uh—your creativity."

"My hats, you mean? I thought you didn't appreciate my creativity."

"I applauded, didn't I? First time I've ever willingly witnessed a fashion show and applauded voluntarily."

Their number was called and Hitch went to get their order and bring it to the table. The next few minutes were taken up with salt and ketchup and extra creamer for the coffee.

"So," Cindy said after she'd taken the edge off her appetite, "idea number one is that I needed something to boot me out of the nest, right? I distinctly remember telling you that I planned to leave as soon as the wedding was over and Maura got off to New York, and—"

"Look me in the eye and tell me you would actually walk out and leave your aunt all alone in that big house. Go ahead, I want to hear it."

"I—well, of course I wouldn't go until she could find someone to come in a few days a week. Maybe even some sort of a companion. She's not really old, but she's sort of—um—dependent?"

"Right. And how long do you think it would take her to find someone willing to work for the same wages you were paid?"

"But I wasn't—I didn't—" She dismissed it with a wave of her hand and took another big bite of her all-the-way cheeseburger. When she could speak again, she said, "All right, point to you. You mentioned two ideas?"

"I did?" Reaching out, he removed a bit of mustard from the corner of her mouth. It felt incredibly intimate, his touching her mouth that way. Cindy told herself not to be foolish, not to start dreaming again. Or at least if she dreamed, to stick to practical, achievable dreams that didn't depend on anyone but herself.

"Okay, idea number two is to establish a base of operations until you can figure out your next move. A bus station is no place to map out a future, agreed?"

She nodded. The idea hadn't appealed to her, either, but she hadn't known what else to do.

"Right. You don't have a particular destination in mind, no prospects, you've got just enough cash for a few meals and a night or two in a cheap motel. You with me so far?"

She stared at him, wondering if she really wanted to hear this.

"Okay then, here's what I have in mind."

Chapter Seven

"No," she said flatly.

"Yes."

"Give me one good reason why I should." Cindy had been stunned when Hitch had suggested it, but not too stunned to know it was the last thing she needed now. She'd read somewhere that kidnapping victims sometimes grew dependent on their captors. She wasn't being kidnapped, but she was hovering on the brink of being in love with the guy. Living with him, if only for a few days, might push her over the edge. She wasn't about to tell him that.

"How about three good reasons?"

"You and your reasons," she muttered, scowling at her empty coffee cup.

It was late. They were both exhausted. Hitch had spent the morning helping Pop put up shelves in his garage. Her own exhaustion was more emotional than physical, but it still packed a wallop.

"Hey, I'm an engineer. It's the way we work."

"Well, I'm a hat designer. The creative process has more to do with instinct and impressions than it does with reason, and right now my instinct tells me this is not going to work. As for my impression..." Frowning slightly, she stroked the smooth, warm crockery.

"Go on. Your impression?" he prompted.

She forced herself to meet his gaze. He had her best interests at heart, she reminded herself. He also had a guileless look on his face that she didn't quite trust. In fact, she was beginning to believe that when it came to men, she wasn't nearly as smart as she'd thought, despite growing up with Maura and Steff. Cindy had been witness to any number of sisterly exchanges concerning hunks and studs and the varying degrees thereof, but when it came to Hitch, who was probably in a class by himself in both categories, she hadn't a clue.

"I'll tell you my impressions after you tell me your three reasons why I should go home with you."

"Deal. Reason number one—you're bushed. We both are. It's been quite a day, one way and another, so what we both need is a good night's sleep, right?"

Tentatively, she nodded.

"Second, if you dig into your funds for a motel and breakfast, you won't have enough left to operate. Any decent rooming house is going to charge you a deposit and a month's rent before you even move in. Are you willing to accept a loan?"

She scowled at him. He pressed his advantage. "Cindy, I don't think you've got much choice."

"I don't believe in going into debt. I already owe Maura whatever the earrings cost above what I gave her."

"Just out of curiosity, how much did you give her?"

Sighing, Cindy decided he already knew every embarrassing thing there was to know about her except that one of her feet was half a size smaller than the other. "My savings totaled $372.57. I wrote her a check for $350. I had some cash in my wallet, and I left a little in the account in case the bank has some fees or charges, or something."

Hitch paused for a count of ten. It didn't help a whole lot. He'd seen day-old chicks with better survival instincts. "I take it you got a receipt?"

She shook her head slowly. "I'll have my canceled check. Oh, and that reminds me, I'd better see about getting my mail forwarded once I get an address."

"We'll handle that. Did you ask to see a sales slip for the earrings? Something to prove they're worth three hundred and fifty bucks?"

"Certainly not. Maura said they were a gift from her daddy. Uncle Henry was generous that way. There's no way I can replace the sentimental value, but they were big gray pearls surrounded by diamonds set in white gold in a square design."

"Sounds gaudy."

"Well…they sort of were. And I like gaudy, you know I do, only those weren't—well, they weren't my style of gaudy, if you know what I mean."

Reaching across the table, he covered her hand with his own. "Yeah, I think I'm getting to recognize your style. Okay, so the bottom line is you handed over your entire fortune for no good reason except you thought you owed it.''

"That's not entirely true. I don't *owe* it because I really did put the earrings where I said I did, only they weren't there, and since I was the last one to see them, I'm responsible.''

"Right. I see your logic. I think.''

"Speaking of logic…'' Cindy covered a yawn with her hand. "You owe me one more reason why I should go home with you.''

"Okay, reason number three is that you're out on your feet.'' He grinned, his tired eyes sparkling like wet slate. "Maybe not your feet, but I'd say what you need is a place to hole up, get some rest, give yourself a little time and perspective before you try to come up with a workable plan for the immediate future.''

She yawned again. "That was reason number one, restated.''

"Don't get technical, you're a hat maker, remember?''

"Hat designer. You still owe me another reason, but I'm too tired to argue now.''

Smugly, he held out a hand, and she took it and got to her feet. "Then let's go. I figure I've got just enough caffeine in my system to get us home. Once we get there you can sack up for as long as it takes while I work on the backlog in my office.''

It was midmorning before hunger drove Cindy out of the tiny guest room that obviously doubled as a storage room for dead files, stacks of newspaper clippings, several years' accumulation of technical publications and miscellaneous boxes. The only thing that had interested her when she'd been shown the room the night before had been the narrow, but incredibly comfortable bed and the bathroom between the two bedrooms.

What interested her now was the mesmerizing fragrance of coffee and bacon drifting from the front of the apartment.

She glanced at her watch, amazed that she'd slept so long, not to mention so soundly. She hadn't even dreamed, a rarity in itself. She always dreamed in full color, even though her dreams seldom made sense.

Her plastic bags, one filled with hats and hat materials, the other with her personal belongings, were still where Hitch had left them. Last night she'd dug out a pair of pajamas and a toothbrush. Now she rummaged for a hairbrush and something that wasn't too horribly wrinkled. She wasn't sure he owned an iron; even his blue jeans looked as though they'd been run through one of those ironing machines at a laundry.

She might have taken the time to locate her suitcase if Maura hadn't been right on her heels every minute. Her hats would have had to be bagged, anyway, because there was no way she could carry so many boxes. As for her clothes, she'd have felt slightly foolish at her age carrying a child's cardboard suitcase with cartoon characters on it, but at least she could have folded a few things instead of dumping them all into one plastic bag.

Although by now, Aunt S. had probably given the

suitcase to Goodwill, along with the toys Cindy had brought with her when she'd first gone to live with the Stephensons. She'd cried for weeks over that.

But that was the past and she was on the verge of the future, so she shook out a denim skirt and yellow camp shirt she'd bought at a discount store on sale. It would have to do for job hunting, which was her first priority. She'd deliberately left most of her hand-me-downs behind.

"Breakfast call, get a move on!"

Even the sound of Hitch's voice did funny things to her nerves. Last night she'd been too tired to fully appreciate what she'd let herself in for. This morning there was no avoiding the truth. She was walking a tightrope here. If Hitch ever realized how she felt about him, she would wither up and die of embarrassment. There was nothing so pathetic as being in love with someone who considered you his good deed of the day.

"I'll wash dishes," she said when she saw the condition of his kitchen. Bacon grease was spattered all over the range top. There were eggshells and bread crumbs on the counter, and dirty dishes everywhere. He might be a terrific design engineer, but a housekeeper he was not.

"No problem, I've got a—"

"I insist."

He shrugged. "Well, sure, but don't feel like you have to do it. Cooking for two's no more trouble than cooking for one, and I always eat a big breakfast."

She got out the juice, checked the sell-by date; it was a few days overdue, but probably safe. There was a jar of apple butter in the refrigerator, and she took out that along with the half-and-half, which was on the verge of going bad, but she had to have something to dilute her coffee. It looked strong enough to do push-ups.

"Have another slice of bacon." He shoved it onto her plate and took the last slice himself. "I've been doing some thinking."

"Me, too."

Ignoring her, he said, "The thing is, I can't see any sense in paying money you don't have for a room you don't need when I've got a perfectly good bed going to waste." He looked at her then, really looked, making her painfully aware of her shortcomings. She had tamed her hair for the time being, but there wasn't one blooming thing she could do about a face full of freckles, short of a layer or two of latex paint. "How'd you sleep?" he asked solicitously.

"Like a log. I'm surprised you didn't hear the sound of sawing wood."

Rising, he refilled both cups. He moved the way she imagined an athlete would, with all his various body parts working in smooth unison. Arm bone connected to the shoulder bone, shoulder bone connected to the backbone, backbone connected to the hip bone, hip bone connected to the...

Well.

And she liked the way he smelled, too. Sort of clean and masculine—shaving soap with overtones of bacon and coffee. She closed her eyes and inhaled appreciatively, then opened them quickly when he spoke.

"Okay, here's the plan. I'll be spending most of the time at the office, clearing out the backlog, getting ready to tackle a couple of new projects. I usually get in late, watch the news and turn in. Which means you'll pretty much have the place to yourself. You can check out the classifieds, call around, make a list of all the possibilities, jobwise and roomwise, and we'll work out transportation later. Meanwhile, you won't be digging into your capital. Does that sound reasonable?"

"For my part it sounds marvelous, but what do you get out of all this?"

"A star in my crown?" The comment came with another quirky grin. Cindy wondered if there was enough armor in the world to protect her from his disarming brand of charm.

"How about I do the cooking and cleaning, and promise not to run up any long distance bills on your phone?" she bargained. "I'll chip in for groceries and—"

"How about two out of the four."

They argued and bargained, and in the end Cindy couldn't have said who won. She was sensible enough to know she hadn't a whole lot of choice. She was also sensible enough to recognize quicksand when she was up to her neck and sinking fast.

Half an hour later Hitch collected his briefcase and left for the office, after first directing her attention to a couple of ads. Without mentioning the exorbitant surcharge, he gave her the number of a grocer who delivered, and suggested she order whatever she thought they needed. Made it sound as if she'd be doing him a favor, when the truth was he honestly preferred to eat out, except for breakfast. Today he'd had coffee at seven, then waited for her to wake up before cooking breakfast.

Tomorrow he'd get back on schedule.

When he reached his office, the first thing he did was to call his twice-a-week housekeeper to tell her he'd let her know when her services were needed again. Mrs. Murphey had more clients than she could handle; he wasn't as afraid of doing her out of a job as he was of doing himself out of a dependable housekeeper.

As if he didn't have other commitments, he spent a couple of hours working on an inexpensive hands-free telephone. Murphey had given him the idea when she'd complained about trying to hold a telephone in one hand and leaf through a catalog or take notes with the other. He'd bought her a speaker phone, but in his spare time he liked to toy with other possibilities.

When he could put it off no longer he dialed his parents' number. The machine picked up after the second ring. Even with an unlisted number, his parents preferred to screen their calls. He left a message saying he was back in Richmond and he'd call again in a few days. Dutiful son stuff. Guilty conscience stuff.

Well, hell, he couldn't please 'em all. At least he was pulling samaritan duty where it really counted. He hated to think about where Cindy would have ended up if he hadn't happened to be there when the fan got hit.

* * *

His partner left early for his sister's kid's birthday party. The secretary they shared left at five. The rest of the staff worked out of their homes.

Hitch stayed until seven, hoping to minimize his exposure to what was waiting for him at home. Usually on Murphey's days, there'd be a casserole waiting to be nuked. On other days he either stopped at his favorite steak house or picked up a pizza. If there was a ball game, he'd snare a beer from the fridge, shed his coat, tie and shoes, kick back and dine in style.

He'd first taken an interest in sports back when his parents had started dragging him to concerts, operas and plays. He'd still been in short pants at the time. A few years later that early interest had paid off in a football scholarship. That had been the start of his open rebellion.

Now, all these years later, he had a comfortable, custom-tailored life-style, which might be selfish, but dammit, it was his life. His business was starting to take off. He had as much or as little social life as he wanted, and whenever his conscience got the best of him he'd drive to Lynchburg and visit his parents, after first making an appointment.

Oh, yeah, he had this bachelor thing down pat. The thing that bothered him now was how Cindy was going to fit in.

How long was he going to have to mind his manners? If one of his parents happened to call, as they occasionally did—maybe once or twice a year— what would they think when a woman answered?

And what the devil did he care? He was thirty-four years old, fully self-supporting and independent. If he wanted to keep a dozen women, it was nobody's business but his own.

He pictured Cindy the way he'd left her this morning, curled up in the lopsided leather chair he refused to toss out even though the thing was ugly as homemade sin. She'd been frowning down at the classifieds, searching for the magic words that would launch her and her wacky hats into an unsuspecting world.

Ah, honey, I hate to be the one to break it to you, but it's not quite that easy, he thought as he pulled into the parking lot behind the three-story brick apartment house.

First thing tomorrow he'd set his secretary to helping Cindy find a place she could afford—something safe, clean, in a decent neighborhood. And then he'd arrange to pay the freight up front without letting her know about it.

Yeah, and pigs would fly. The lady was naive; she wasn't stupid.

The first thing that greeted him when he unlocked his door was a smell that reminded him of Mama Mac. Pot roast. Mrs. Kueber, his mother's cook and housekeeper, had never, to his knowledge, cooked a pot roast.

"Oh, hi! I didn't know what time to expect you, so I cooked something that would keep."

She was barefooted. She had a pencil stuck in her hair. She was wearing baggy jeans and a T-shirt that was knotted at her waist. With a folded newspaper in her hand, she looked about sixteen years old.

Trouble was, he knew better. He knew how her head worked; she might be a bit unrealistic, but there was nothing at all immature about either her brain or her body.

"Aw, honey, you didn't have to do that."

"I wanted to. I ordered it first thing this morning, and it's no trouble to cook. I've circled lots of for-rents in the paper, and a couple of jobs, but I thought I'd better ask you first."

The whole place gleamed. It smelled the way it did when Murphey got done with her bimonthly scrub-down. Hell, even his favorite long-legged spider had been dispossessed.

"Well? Aren't you going to say something?"

She had that look he was coming to know all too well. Arms crossed, back stiff, jaw set, eyes glittering with determination. He was coming to know her almost as well as he knew himself. Knew her strengths and her weaknesses—even shared a few of each, if the truth be known.

She could make him laugh like no one else he'd ever known. She could also exasperate him faster than anyone else he knew—with the possible exception of his mother. But that wasn't the real problem. The real problem was that Cindy could also turn him on quicker than any woman he'd ever known. Even barefooted, in baggy jeans and a sagging T-shirt, she radiated a kind of natural sexuality that she probably wasn't even aware of.

He was. It was downright scary. She wasn't his usual type. Hell, he didn't even have a type, but if he had, it wouldn't have been Cindy Danbury.

"Well?" she repeated, those guileless eyes of hers gently taking him apart.

"Smells good," he allowed cautiously. After

shedding his jacket, he unbuttoned the top two buttons on his shirt and tried to pick his way through a minefield he hadn't anticipated. Should have, but hadn't.

Evidently he managed to strike the right note. Some of the starch went out of her and she picked up his jacket and hung it in the closet.

"You don't have to do that."

"Oh. Shall I hang it back on the chair, then?" She half turned toward him, the soft knit of her shirt tightening across her small breasts. If she wore a bra, it was a thin one. He could see her nipples. Tired though he was, his body reacted with embarrassing enthusiasm.

"Do anything you damn well want to," he snapped, and could have bitten off his tongue. He saw her stiffen, watched the wariness creep back into her eyes, and shook his head. "Look, I'm sorry, okay? We're going to have to work out a few ground rules. First, I'm not used to sharing my space. In case you hadn't noticed, I tend to be a bit of a slob."

Not a word. Not so much as a flicker of an eyelash. He knew the signs, remembered them from years ago when his parents had tried every tactic they knew, from bribery to guilt, to turn him into the kind of son they wanted. The kind he was supposed to be, had been programmed to become, only something had gone haywire. He'd been a disappointment from the time he'd first announced his decision to try out for Little League instead of spending his summers at the approved summer camp, with the approved sons of his parents' approved colleagues.

"How about if I back out and we start over?"

After a moment she laughed, and he was reminded all over again of what it was about her that made her dangerous.

Things like her looks, her quick smile, that husky laugh of hers. The way she whistled when she worked, the way she smelled, the way she tasted, the way she thought...

Hitch didn't know what it all added up to, but he did know that for a man who was averse to close involvements of a personal nature, she was off-limits. With his parents as an example of marital bliss, plus the fact that more than half his friends had been divorced at least once, he wasn't about to get caught in that particular trap. No way.

"I believe you said dinner was ready? Give me ten minutes to wash up and change, and we'll dish it up together, shall we?"

She beamed as if he'd offered her a present on Christmas morning. It shouldn't be that easy. He was going to have to teach her a few defensive moves before he let her out into the real world.

He was back in five, his face and hands damp, hair neatly combed, dressed in his oldest khakis and a black knit shirt. He was barefoot, too. He knew she didn't have very much if, as he suspected, one of those lumpy sacks of hers was full of hats.

She'd changed, too. Wearing the denim skirt and a yellow cotton shirt again, plus a pair of tan moccasins and a touch of lipstick, she still looked like a teenager, which made him feel guilty as sin for what he was thinking.

But the beef was outstanding, and he told her so. She smiled and ladled another serving of potatoes, carrots and gravy onto his plate. "So," he said, helping himself to his third roll, "you said you found a few promising leads today?"

"Three," she said. "Jobs, that is. I thought I'd better check out addresses with you first when it comes to rooms for rent."

"Good thinking. We'll sort out the jobs first, maybe even check out a few before we think about a place to live. Agreed?"

After only the briefest hesitation, she nodded. Suddenly, he wasn't sure she was quite as easy to read as he'd thought. The lady had a mind of her own, all right. One that hadn't come with a schematic.

They adjourned to the living room, leaving the dishes on the table until later. Cindy objected; Hitch insisted. He made the mistake of placing a hand on her back to steer her through the door and immediately regretted it. There was nothing faintly sexy about the outfit she was wearing, but the lady herself was something else.

Delicate was the first word that came to mind. Through the crisp cotton shirt and whatever she wore underneath, her body felt warm and delicate and strong, and he wanted to do more than touch her back.

Which was one more reason to get her settled and

out of his life as quickly as possible. At a safe distance, they might even maintain a friendship.

Or maybe not. He wasn't so sure there was such a thing as a safe distance where Cindy was concerned.

Chapter Eight

It didn't take a genius to know that this wasn't working for either of them, Cindy acknowledged to herself the second morning. She closed the door behind Hitch, the scent of his bergamot aftershave setting off all sorts of inappropriate thoughts, and told herself that one way or another she had to find a job that paid enough so that she could move out before it was too late.

Not even to herself would she dare define "too late."

Maybe she could find a woman's support group and throw herself on their mercy. There had to be something of the sort in a city as large as Richmond.

"Help, please," she could say. "I'm head over heels crazy in love with the guy I'm living with and if I don't get help I might throw myself at his head and beg him to take me!"

And he, of course, being a gentleman, would politely decline, and she'd go to her grave untaken, because if Hitch wouldn't take her, no other man would be offered the chance.

At any other time, given her present state of frustration, she'd have dragged out all her old forties fashion magazines, with their wonderful hats, and started sketching. But she'd left them behind, along with her collection of Gibson Girl pictures, because nothing weighed more than stacks of paper.

She would simply have to start collecting all over again. Besides, it wasn't as if she hadn't memorized every hat Lily Dache had ever created, or every drawing that Charles Gibson had ever done of an elegant, wasp-waisted woman with a skinny little neck, an enormous coiffure and an even more impressive hat.

Shoulders drooping, Cindy wondered, not for the first time, why she couldn't have been born with a perfectly ordinary ambition to become…well, why not a concert musician? She couldn't sing or play an instrument, but she could whistle really well.

Or an inventor, like her father?

Hitch was right. Nobody wore her kind of hats anymore. She might pile neon-colored daisies on a baseball cap and catch someone's attention, but barring that, she'd just as well hibernate and wait out the next few fashion cycles until big, flowery, feminine hats came back in style again.

Trouble was, being a hat designer wasn't a choice, it was a calling. Something she'd been born with, like a passion for chocolate covered cherries, or bagpipes. The first doll she ever remembered owning had come from the Dollar Store, but Felicia—she'd named her for her Sunday School teacher—Felicia had owned more hats than Barbie, for all *her* sophistication, had ever dreamed of.

"So...time to get real, lady," Cindy said aloud. "The first person who offers you a dime more than minimum wage gets you, no matter what the job is."

Having lived on the charity of others since she was a child, she knew her first priority was independence. The hats could wait. They'd waited this long; another few years wouldn't matter.

Another few decades probably wouldn't matter, but she refused to fall prey to negative thinking. Someday hats would come back again in all their glory, and when they did she'd be waiting with a warehouse full of Chapeaux by Cynthia.

Between an appointment with a garden tractor manufacturer who wanted to appeal to a more feminine market, and an appointment with his optometrist, Hitch studied the classifieds. Then he placed a call to the agency that had found him both the perfect secretary and the perfect housekeeper.

"She's artistic, creative—she can do most anything and do it well, and— Computer skills? No, I don't think so."

Absently, he massaged with his thumb a place between his eyebrows. "Yeah—well, no. That is, I don't believe she's ever done any—"

He sighed, opened a drawer, fumbled with one hand for the aspirin he kept there and said, "Yeah, I know, but I thought I'd give you a heads up so you can start— Right. I'll bring her in first thing tomorrow—okay, then Monday, and we'll—that is, she'll do your paperwork, but meanwhile, if you think of anything, keep us in mind, will you?"

Dinner was fried chicken. She met him at the door gnawing on a wing, and started apologizing almost immediately.

"Oh, my, I bet you like wings best, don't you? There's another one, and two of everything else, and I cut the breast into four pieces. They're small, but—"

"Cindy."

"And I made stuffed potato shells. All I have to do is pop them in the—"

"Cindy, quit trying so damned hard, will you?"

She wilted before his eyes. If he'd smacked her in the face with a wet raincoat the effect couldn't have been more profound. "Look, I've had a rotten day, my head's hurting and I'm—"

Starving, he'd been about to say.

"I'm sorry. I know I talk too much, everybody says so, so why don't I just dish up supper and leave you to it? I—I've already eaten." She waved the half-gnawed chicken wing, her smile as false as it was fleeting.

You're a bastard, Hitchcock. Why not toss her out into the snowstorm and be done with it?

Because the temperature was in the eighties, for one thing. Because what he wanted more than anything at this moment was to lie down and hold her in his arms until the aspirin did their thing, and then eat whatever she'd cooked while he told her about his day and she told him about hers.

Which just went to show that he'd finally lost it.

Flat out lost whatever common sense he'd been born with, which wasn't, according to his father, enough to bring him in out of the rain.

"Give me a few minutes, will you? Then why don't we take trays into the living room? D'you mind if I watch TV? There's a commercial I want to catch, and then we'll talk."

The chicken was the best he'd ever tasted. He'd probably have to have his arteries reamed out before he was forty, because she admitted she'd fried it in bacon grease, but he ate three pieces, along with two stuffed potato halves and a double serving of green salad to assuage his conscience.

Technically, the commercial was good, but it would have been better if the lawn tractor had looked less like a mechanical praying mantis and more like something a woman could start with a touch and steer with one hand.

Cindy hadn't said a word. She'd hardly eaten anything, he noticed belatedly. Sighing, he shoved his tray aside, stood and collected them both. "I'll bring the coffee and we'll talk, okay?"

She looked wary, as if she'd traveled down this road before. He poured both coffees, fixed hers the way she liked it, and settled back in his chair.

"You found me a job, didn't you?" She got in the first shot.

"What if I said yes?"

"Then I'd say thank you very much for everything and start making arrangements to find a place of my own."

She had to know he'd done no such thing. In the

first place, nobody would hire her, sight unseen, despite all the Help Wanted signs in store windows.

In the second place, he had to be sure it was the right job, one where her unique blend of talents would be appreciated and amply rewarded.

In which case, he thought as he met her uncomfortably direct gaze, she didn't stand a snowball's chance in hell of finding work.

"May I go first?" she asked, putting him instantly on guard.

"Be my guest."

"I am, that's part of the trouble. Your guest, I mean." A quiver of a smile followed her words, triggering a whole new set of doubts on his part. Dammit, he couldn't just let her go. She was too…too special. Too fragile.

Yeah, about as fragile as a steel butterfly.

"Believe it or not, there's a place here that manufactures hats," Cindy continued. "They're mostly sporty things for men, with team names on them, but it would be a start. I called."

"And?" His headache was suddenly worse. He rubbed the spot between his eyebrows where headaches always seemed to focus.

"And they have an opening in the shipping department."

"Jeez, Cindy, you're not going to work in any damn shipping department! You'd be on your feet all day long."

As if he hadn't interrupted, she went on talking. "For someone with no experience, I'm not sure the starting pay would be enough to live on, with all the withholding. I'd forgotten about that."

And he'd forgotten just how naive she was. "Have you ever held a paying job? Besides your Monday thing, I mean?"

Her gaze shifted. "No, not really."

"After I give you a crash course on survival, why don't we talk to this agency I know? I made an appointment for Monday, and the head of the agency, who happens to be a personal friend of mine, promised to check around for something along the lines of what you're looking for."

"I found a hat job on my own," she said defensively.

Why was it that every time he looked at her he wanted to reach out and touch her? Hold her?

Trouble was, it wouldn't stop at holding and touching. Even with a grinding headache, his libido was awake and raring to go.

Down, boy. Have you no sense of decorum?

He'd heard that a few thousand times, too, if not quite for the same reason. His parents had always been big on decorum.

"Let's give it some time, shall we? You don't have to grab the first thing that comes along. If it doesn't suit, and you quit after the first week, it won't look good on your resumé."

"I don't have a resumé."

"That's another thing we need to work on this weekend."

"You mean what I need is to make a record of how many times I took Miss Emma to the beauty shop and how many times I cleaned Arvilla Davis's bird cages?" Cindy made a sound of disgust with her tongue and teeth that had him staring in fascination at her mouth. It had been what—three days? four?—since he'd kissed her?

Hitch found he was hungry for that mouth all over again. Pleading a headache, he turned in early and then lay awake half the night wondering if he was in over his head. If he could get out without doing any damage. If he even wanted to get out....

The next day was Saturday. He didn't have to go to the office, but he went anyway. It was safer than hanging around all day, watching her clean an apartment that was already spotless because she insisted on earning her keep.

He managed to stay away until midafternoon, thus reducing his exposure. Came home to find her ironing his pajamas, which he'd slept in only because she was here.

"Well, hi," she said brightly. Her face was almost as red as her hair. He wasn't sure if it was from exertion or embarrassment, and thought he'd probably be better off not asking. "Did you know there's a perfectly good washer and dryer right here in the building? Your downstairs neighbor told me about it. She said it's for the use of the tenants, so I gathered up what I could find and—"

"Dammit, Cindy, that's three flights of stairs! Four, if you count the basement." His apartment was on the third floor. He'd never even seen the basement.

"Well, she said not to trust the elevator because it hangs up sometimes, and besides, I needed the exercise. I'm not used to doing nothing."

Raking a hand though his hair, he said, "You call

this nothing? Dammit, Cindy, I didn't bring you here to put you to work. At least, not for me.''

"Did you know you curse an awful lot? I don't remember you doing that before, when I used to—''

He dropped his briefcase and unbuttoned the neck of his knit shirt. On Saturdays he never dressed. No reason to. He never made business appointments on weekends. "Before what?" he challenged.

"Well, you know...before.''

"No, I don't know. Why don't you tell me?''

"Before, when I used to see you next door show-ing off for Steff and Maura and all those other girls. You used to brag some, but I don't remember hear-ing you curse." She flashed him that elfin grin that never failed to throw him off balance, and said, "You probably knew Mama Mac would've washed your mouth out with soap.''

"Is that how you got your kicks in those days?" he teased. "Peeping through keyholes?''

"Through hedges. No keyholes.''

Thank God for that. While he couldn't remember any X-rated activities offhand, he did recall a lot of showing off, trying to impress the girls and to bed any who were willing.

On second thought, there might have been one or two questionable episodes out on the side porch after the Macs had turned in. Maybe a few more in the cars parked haphazardly along the driveway.

"If you want to know the truth, I was jealous," she admitted. "I wanted to be older and prettier and wear the kind of clothes that made boys notice me.''

"I noticed you," he lied valiantly.

"Sure you did. You even smiled at me once and asked me how it was going."

"And what did you say?" He didn't actually remember it, but he probably had.

"I imagine I turned red in the face and ran away. My social graces weren't much to brag about back then."

"Neither were mine, but by then I'd learned how to fake it."

He was doing his best to put her at ease, but watching the way the sunlight slid through the window, making her hair look like spun copper, her skin like velvet, was having the opposite effect on him. He wondered if she was freckled all over, and remembered wondering the same thing a few times before.

They talked a little longer without ever getting back to the subject of finding her a job and a place to live. Hitch was struck by how easy she was to talk to. Not like other women he'd dated.

Not that he was dating her. She was too young for him, in the first place, and in the second place...

Yeah, Hitchcock, what about that second place?

Once again Hitch deliberately reminded himself of the reasons he'd vowed never to marry. His parents' marriage was enough to sour anyone on the institution. Add to that the fact that he had far too many friends who'd married young, then divorced after a few years, and were now struggling to support two households and fighting bitterly over kids.

No way would he risk that. He had a comfortable life-style, an exciting career and a social life that suited him to a T. He'd worked hard to achieve all this, and he had no intention of throwing it away. Not now. Not ever. Not if he had anything to say about it.

Trouble was, he'd never realized what an insidious thing coming home to a warm, attractive, sexy, funny woman and a delicious home-cooked meal could be. If he had, he'd have left Cindy at the bus station and hightailed it out of town.

No, he wouldn't. Talk about getting caught in a trap of his own design.

He went out Saturday night, claiming a previous engagement. She told him there was a movie on TV she wanted to watch, but not to worry, it wasn't a pay channel.

He uttered another oath and then had to apologize. She was cramping his style in a big way, he told himself, and then admitted that she was right. He'd done very little cursing before she'd erupted into his life again.

He hung out at a sports bar, watching a game he wasn't interested in and drinking beer. When the teams were still tied after twelve innings, he set his fourth beer back on the counter, half-finished, and called a cab. He could collect his car tomorrow.

She was wearing another of her seemingly endless supply of T-shirts. This one was red with a tennis logo on the pocket. Another one of Maura's, no doubt. There was a stain on one shoulder, which explained why it had been passed on.

"How's the movie?"

"It was wonderful," she said softly, her eyes glowing.

"Thought you'd be in bed by now."

"I wanted to be sure you got home all right. Not that you wouldn't, but you waited up for me, remember?"

"Aw, hell, Cindy, I wish you hadn't," he growled.

She shrugged. "I wasn't sleepy, anyway. I looked through some of your books."

Bracing his hands on the back of the leather recliner, he took a deep, steadying breath and wished he hadn't had that last half beer. Or the one before it. He was a two-brew man. One shot of whiskey or two beers—that was his self-imposed limit. For some reason tonight he'd felt compelled to break the rule.

"Hitch? Are you all right?" Her voice was like her laughter, softer, huskier than you'd expect from a feisty redhead with a hair-trigger temper.

Not that he'd seen any evidence of her temper. Maybe he'd just assumed it because she'd lit into him that first day, when he'd nearly run her down on the street.

"Yeah, I'm all right. Go to bed, Cindy."

"Well…if you're sure."

"Just go to bed, will you?"

"Is it another headache?" she persisted.

Lifting his head, he glared at her. "No, dammit, it's not another headache, it's an ache you don't even want to know about!"

"I might be able to help."

It was pure wickedness, the thoughts that ran though his mind then. He'd had a little too much to drink—he'd long ago learned his personal limits, and tonight he had deliberately gone over them—but it wasn't the beer that prompted him to take her up on her offer. "Yeah, I guess maybe you can, at that. Come here."

"Where?" Her eyes had that deer-in-the-headlights look, but she stood her ground.

"Right here, where you can put your hands on where it hurts."

Aw, jeez, I can't believe I said that! That is so cheesy!

She moved closer, but looked ready to take off at the first sign of danger. "Where does it hurt?"

He couldn't go through with it. Not with Cindy. Either he wasn't drunk enough or he wasn't enough of a bastard, so he sighed and offered her the best smile he could summon, given the circumstances.

That was when she made her mistake. She touched him. On the shoulder, with her face tipped up so that she could look in his eyes and see what ailed him.

She could have looked lower and found out a lot quicker.

"You should've run when you had the chance," he told her just before he wrapped her in his arms and lowered his face to hers.

Chapter Nine

At least, Hitch told himself later—much later—
he'd had sense enough not to take her into the bedroom. What happened had happened spontaneously,
not through any design.

Not through any *conscious* design, he amended.

He had kissed her before. Careful little kisses that
did no harm and weren't in any danger of getting
out of hand because he'd deliberately chosen a safe
time and place.

A public park.

The front porch, in full view of anyone driving
past.

The side yard, in that crazy jungle she called a
garden.

But now they were in his apartment. Alone together, late at night. And while he wasn't drunk, or
anywhere near it, he'd had enough to take the ra-
zor's edge off his judgment. Enough to know that

he was making a mistake. Enough to go ahead and make it anyway.

So he kissed her.

"This isn't smart," was all the warning he offered.

"I know," she whispered, her breath mingling with his.

Incendiary was the word that came to mind when he fought his way to the surface again. If a few beers could screw up his judgment, this woman was the equivalent of a three-day binge. They were sprawled on the sofa, Cindy on her back, with him lying half on top of her. The sofa was barely wide enough for one adult, much less two. It was not a situation designed for rational thought, and for the life of him he couldn't remember how they got there.

"You okay?"

She was breathing hard. So was he. "I don't think so," she gasped.

"I'm too heavy," he said. He tried to ease off her, but when she dug her fingers into his shoulders, he hoisted the white flag and stayed where he was. One more minute, he warned his raging hormones—that's all you get, so cool down, Hitchcock.

His hand was still on her breast. Under her T-shirt. She wasn't wearing a bra. He could feel her nipple, hard as a tiny acorn, nudging his palm.

Oboy.

"Honey, I'm afraid I've been drinking," he growled softly.

"I know."

"Lousy excuse. Worse excuse in the world."

"I know."

"I didn't bring you here to take advantage of you." Still making lame excuses. God, he was pathetic.

"I know."

It started to get to him then—her all-knowingness. "Well, if you know so much, why'd you kiss me back?" he demanded, regretting the words before they were even out.

No wonder he'd never managed to live up to his parents' expectations. "Cindy, I'm sorry. This is all my fault—I should never have brought you here." He eased his thigh off hers and sat up, partly because he was still uncomfortably aroused and it wasn't going to get any better until he put some space between them. Maybe a couple of counties would do it.

It was a damned undignified situation for a man of his age, making out on the living room sofa, going at it hot and heavy.

"It's not your fault," she said, so quietly that at first he didn't even hear her, he was so caught up in his own miserable half excuses. "I wanted you to kiss me, and when you did, I didn't want you to stop, but you're right. It's not smart."

"Did I say that? Yeah, I guess I did." He tried to tell himself that she wanted it as much as he did. They were both adults, neither of them committed to anyone else. But it didn't work. What she needed now was a friend, not a lover.

And what do you need, Hitchcock?

Don't ask.

Cindy shivered. Physically he was still here, but he obviously didn't want to be. She could sense his withdrawal before he ever moved away. Even if they made love and then a miracle happened and he proposed to her, she couldn't accept. Hitch didn't want marriage any more than she did. They both appreciated freedom too much.

And for the first time in her life, she reminded herself, her own freedom was within reach. She would think of that, and not the way he'd touched her breasts until she went clean out of her mind. Not the way he'd touched her between her thighs and she'd lifted her hips and pressed herself shamelessly against his hand.

Face facts, woman. Or as Maura says, get real!

"First thing tomorrow I intend to find a job and a room, and then I'll be off your hands. It's what I intended to do all along. What I want more than anything. Independence," she added, in case he was still feeling trapped.

He stood and tucked in his shirttail, reminding her of how it had come to be out. She had stroked him all over, front and back, feeling the intricate structure of his back muscles and his chest muscles—all those pecs and abs and whatever that the exercise people always talked about.

She'd been amazed to discover that his nipples were as sensitive as hers. She'd touched him there and felt them stiffen, heard him gasp as if she'd stuck him with a hat pin. Regardless of how much she'd thought she knew, she still had a lot to learn about men.

"I'll lock up," he said, which was purely unnecessary, because the door locked automatically unless you turned the little whatchamacallit. And she hadn't.

"Fine. I'll fix the coffeepot for morning."

Also unnecessary. He'd made his own morning coffee long before she'd come on the scene. He'd go on making it long after she was only a dim memory.

She thought she might cry. Gulping hard, she fled.

Actually, she did cry a little, something she seldom indulged in because it clogged up her nose and made her throat ache. But she cried for a few minutes, and then she got up and blew her nose and told herself she would leave tomorrow if she had to wash dishes for a living. She might not have much in the way of financial resources, but she had her hats, her pride and her virginity.

For what it was worth.

Which evidently wasn't much, if the only man in the world she'd ever loved wasn't interested in it.

"You're not leaving here today. It's Sunday. The unemployment offices are closed, you don't have enough money—no, don't look at me like that, dammit!"

"I believe I can find a place," she said, her voice as calm and composed as if her stomach weren't threatening to rebel. As a rule when that happened she would picture a plain straw hat and mentally shape it and trim it until she calmed down again and her stomach stopped pumping acid.

Designing hats in her mind wasn't going to get her out of this mess, though. No indeedy. This, as she'd been told more than once, was the real world.

"My secretary has a spare room. She's perfectly willing to let you use it as long as you—"

"No, thank you, I've made other plans."

"The devil you say. What plans? When did you make any plans?"

"What did you think I'd been doing all this time?"

"That's what I'm asking you."

She could hardly tell him that her plans consisted of a list of economy motels copied from the telephone book—motels didn't require deposits—plus the morning's Help Wanted ads and a brand-new idea inspired by a radio commercial she'd heard while she was making the beds.

"If you must know, there's a flea market going on," she said, her whole attitude one of defiance.

"What's the fee?"

"The fee?"

"The fee. How much does it cost to rent a table?"

The defiance leaked out like helium from a punctured balloon. "You have to rent a table?"

"Haven't you ever been to one of those things?"

"Of course I have. Dozens of them. I've even helped out." His mouth looked grim this morning, but it was the same mouth, she reminded herself, that had thoroughly explored her own and then kissed its way down to her breasts only a few hours ago.

He was obviously waiting for a response. Reining in her imagination, she told him that the church held flea markets twice a year to raise funds. "And the library—"

"This is a commercial affair, not a charity. You

rent space and sell whatever you've got to sell. Not that it's any of my business, but just what did you intend to sell?''

She pressed her hand against her stomach. Milk, she thought as panic began to set in. Maybe even half-and-half.

"Well?" he prompted when she hesitated.

"My hats."

He tipped back his head and closed his eyes. He'd been pacing for the past few minutes while she sat in a kitchen chair, trying to pretend she was somewhere else—anywhere else—and that her stomach wasn't hurting and that none of this was happening.

"Ah, hell, Cindy—dammit!"

"Stop cursing. You're intelligent enough to express yourself without profanity."

"You call what you want to do intelligent? Cindy, you can't sell your hats."

"Why not? They're mine. At least no one's likely to accuse me of—of stealing them."

He massaged the back of his neck and then pinched the place where his eyebrows almost met. He did that a lot, she'd noticed. Tension headaches, probably. And at the moment, she was making them worse, which didn't help her own ailment at all.

They were a pair, all right.

"Why not?" he exclaimed. "Because—because they're your grubstake, that's why not. They're the credentials that are going to launch your career, once you're ready. Because—"

"Because you think nobody would buy them," she finished for him. "They're only cheap beach hats from the dime store, reshaped and trimmed with fake flowers and feathers and cheap glass beads. I know I still have a lot to learn, but there are hat-making classes. I intend to take one, and that will put me in touch with hat people.''

"Hat people," he echoed, shaking his head slowly.

"Look, it's not engineering, okay? It might not sound important or logical or—or even reasonable to you—but fashion is a legitimate career. People have been designing clothes—and hats, too—ever since Eve got tired of wearing the same three fig leaves every day.''

"I'll take your word for it.''

She sat up straighter as the pain in her belly eased slightly. "You don't have to take my word for anything. Just ask yourself why men wear neckties.''

Nonplussed, he glanced down at his tieless shirt. "Because...because—well, actually, there's a very good reason why men wear neckties.''

"And that reason is?'' She waited. She could have told him that his type of engineering wasn't all that logical, either. In fact, it wasn't that far removed from her own field. He made things look better so that they'd sell better. She made things that looked good so that the people who wore them would feel better.

"Uh...to keep gravy off our shirts?''

Laughter was as good a relief valve as any. She laughed, and after the briefest moment, he laughed, too. Some of the tension engendered by latent sexual energy began to ease.

Not that anything had changed. They both knew that this was in all likelihood the last time they would ever share morning coffee in his kitchen. That the friendship that had sprung up so unexpectedly between them and flourished so briefly had no real future.

"So," she said brightly, rising to shove her chair back under the table. "I guess I'd better get started."

He opened his mouth to argue—she could actually see the words forming in his mind—but before he could speak, the telephone rang. She was closest, but she let him take it. It was his phone, after all. And he did have a private life, she reminded herself. One that definitely did not include homeless, out-of-work females who latched on to the first poor soul they could find who offered to feed them and give them shelter.

"Are you serious?" he said to whoever was on the other end.

Cindy went to move past him, but he caught her by the shirttail and held her there.

"Did you give her my number? Yeah—she's right here."

Puzzled, Cindy accepted the phone and waited for the other party to speak. She didn't even know who was calling.

"This is terribly embarrassing," said an all too familiar voice, "but I suppose you deserve to know the truth."

"Aunt S.?"

"And I promise you, that girl hasn't heard the last of it, either."

What girl? Cindy wondered, feeling as if she'd

been plopped down in the middle of a fast-paced mystery. *The truth about what?*

Cindy hung up the phone, a dazed look on her face. Aunt S. was wiring her money in care of Hitch's office. Come Monday morning, her entire fortune would be restored.

"I'm sure Maura didn't know," Cindy said, knowing no such thing. Lorna Stephenson had had the missing earrings all along. Seeing them tossed casually aside, she had taken them with her to teach her youngest daughter a lesson. Even though they were only cultured pearls and cubic zirconia, worth a fraction of what Maura had claimed, they'd been a gift from her father and, as such, were not to be treated carelessly.

"She knew," Hitch stated flatly.

Morosely, Cindy nodded. Of course she'd known. Maura tended to be spiteful, not to mention greedy. Cindy had actually heard her telling Steff that as Steff would have a place in the mountains, Maura would get Hitch to buy them a place at the beach. "It'll be perfect," she'd crowed, as if Hitch would have nothing to say about the matter. As if she and Hitch were an item.

But Hitch hadn't gone along with the plan. Cindy doubted if he even knew about it. He'd been nice to all the women—aunts, cousins, bridesmaids, even Cindy herself—but to her knowledge, he hadn't singled out any one of them for special attention. If anything, he'd actually avoided Maura, which might explain why she'd pitched a royal fit when she'd seen them together.

* * *

Hitch claimed catch-up work at the office as a reason for leaving shortly after lunch. "Take a break. You've been going flat out since before the wedding. If we're going job hunting tomorrow, you need to be on your toes."

"I'd better do some ironing. My interview outfit looks like the dog's been sleeping on it."

They were walking on eggshells, trying to pretend they hadn't made love only hours earlier. Not the whole act. They hadn't gone quite that far, but as far as Cindy was concerned it was love they had made.

He was wearing a black knit shirt with khakis, his standard weekend attire. He couldn't have looked any sexier, she told herself, if he'd been wearing a loincloth.

"Be sure and turn the night latch," he reminded her. "Oh, and by the way—if your stomach's still bothering you, check the medicine cabinet. Liquid or tablets, your choice."

Well, shoot. "Thanks, but I'm fine now." She was better, not fine, but she'd be darned if she would lay another burden on his shoulders, no matter how accommodating they were.

"You're sure?"

She nodded. "By the way, have you thought about having your eyes examined? All those headaches—and I've noticed your arms aren't quite long enough when you're reading."

He swatted her on the behind. She dodged away, then shut the door, leaned against it and sighed. They'd have been so good together. The better she came to know him, the more she realized how much they had in common. They were both creative people, grounded with a broad streak of practicality. They laughed easily together. They liked the same kind of people—the Macs, for instance. And that landscape fellow Hitch had tried to pair her off with. Joe Digby was nice, but her heart was already taken.

It was a good thing, she thought as she gathered up the shirt Hitch had worn the day before and pressed it to her face, inhaling the clean scent of his body—a very good thing they both had the same goal in mind.

By Monday morning Cindy had made her lists, edited them a dozen times and prioritized them. First thing on the list: collect her money and open a bank account. After that, start checking out the job offerings she'd circled in the order they were listed.

Oh, she was good at this. She'd been planning and dreaming for so many years now....

Number three: rent room, weekly basis. That would have to wait until she knew where she'd be working.

"Ready?" Hitch asked. He'd disappeared right after breakfast and reemerged some twenty minutes later, knotting a dark silk tie.

"You look like a gentleman's fashion plate."

Seeing the way she was looking him over, he grinned, indicating the tie. "Shirt-saver securely attached in case of falling gravy."

That wasn't what she'd been thinking about, but it was just as well he couldn't read her mind. "I'm starting to have butterflies," she admitted.

"Don't let 'em bug you."

She rolled her eyes. "Did anyone ever tell you you have a dreadful sense of humor?"

"Takes one to know one," he retorted, and if his intention had been to make her forget her nerves, it worked. If she ever needed an ally, she'd like to have him at her side.

"Sara, meet Cynthia Danbury. Cindy, my invaluable secretary, Sara Ethelbert."

"Oh, you're the hat designer," the dark-haired woman said cheerfully. She looked about Hitch's age, but he'd mentioned that she had a grown son. "I still have all my mother-in-law's hats. I'm dying for hats to come back, but nowadays, people don't even wear them to church. I'd love to see some of yours."

"Sara, did the money come through?"

The woman lifted the phone, pushed the hold button and said, "Yep, right on time. 'Scuse me, this is about that opening I mentioned. Did I forget to mention it? Oh, well, I'll put her through to your office in a minute—and by the way, don't forget to pick up your glasses this morning—they're ready." Turning back to the phone, she said, "Claire? They just walked in."

Hitch shepherded Cindy into the adjoining office and indicated a chair. The room could best be described as organized chaos. There was an intimidating computer and several mysterious machines that she semi-identified as faxes and copiers. There were sketches on the wall, several framed certificates and half a dozen gold-toned sports trophies of varying sizes. She told herself he probably knew where everything in the room was and could lay hands on it at a moment's notice.

"No retail experience," he was saying into the phone when her straying attention returned. "At least nothing formal—yes, I'm sure she could. POS? No problem."

She *who?* What in the world was a POS?

Hitch asked the caller to give him forty-five minutes, and replaced the phone in its cradle. "Sounds promising," he said. "Shows the value of networking." He shed his coat and loosened his tie. "Couple of things I should mention before we go, though. For instance—"

"Wait a minute, if you were referring to me just now, I want to know who that was and what they were talking about, and—and what on earth is this POS you claim is no problem?"

"You want the crash course?" He ticked off the answers on the fingers of his right hand. Nice, long, square-tipped fingers emerging from his nice, square palm.

"The who, first. Personnel department, Marston's Department Store, old family-owned business. Sara happened to know they needed help in the hat department, and when I told her about you, she checked it out with a friend."

"A real hat department?"

Leaning against the cluttered desk, he shrugged. "So I was wrong. Yeah, it happens, even to me. Evidently, a few women still buy hats, so a few stores still sell 'em. Sounds like a good fit to me."

It sounded like a good fit to Cindy, too. Almost

too good. "I…guess so. I expected to be flipping burgers, at least until I could find something better."

He glanced at his wrist. "I'd better fill you in on the way over, before someone else gets hired. If you'd like to freshen up before we go, it's right through there." He indicated a door that held a dartboard and several clippings. Cindy's hand went to her hair, which had probably unraveled on the way to the office. She was painfully conscious of her inappropriate attire, but it was the best she could do. She'd left almost her entire wardrobe of hand-me-downs behind, not wanting any reminders.

She emerged a few minutes later just as Hitch was hanging up the phone. "Ready? On the way, if you don't mind, we'll stop by the optician's and pick up my new glasses. And yes, Miss Know-it-all, my eyes have been giving me headaches, and you needn't say you told me so."

Her smirk said it for her.

Hitch slung his jacket over his shoulder and ushered her out of the office. Sara handed him an envelope on the way out and wished Cindy luck.

She refused to be nervous. She had a strong back, two capable hands and a darned good brain. Today was Monday. Send Cindy had never met the Monday job she couldn't handle.

"Hitch…what's a POS?" she asked on the way down to the parking level.

"Point of sale. It's a system of inventory control."

Her eyes widened. "Oh, my, it's probably a computer thing. Maybe we'd better reevaluate. I can't even set a digital watch, much less operate a computer.''

"Didn't you learn computers in school?''

"Uh...not really. They didn't have enough to go around, and the chairs were really miserable, and my hip was giving me some trouble then, so they let me help out in the library instead.''

"Libraries have computers.''

"Ours did, too, only the librarian was a year from retirement and she didn't want to change to a new system, so we still relied on a card file.''

"Yeah, well—it's not that big a deal. You can write down the key sequence and follow it. You don't have to understand how it works. You'll be fine, honey, believe me.''

She wanted to believe him, she truly did. If any man could sell her the Brooklyn Bridge—or at least, the Yadkin River Bridge—it was John Hale Hitchcock.

Only it wasn't bridges he was selling. He was trying to sell her on herself, and suddenly, she wasn't quite as sure of her own abilities as she would like to be.

He waited until they were seated in the car, and then he turned to her. "Still friends?''

She nodded.

"Trust me?''

She did. Whatever happened today—or didn't happen—she trusted him, so she nodded again.

"Then just between friends, here's one for luck.''

And he kissed her. Lightly, briefly, not lingering, but it was enough to give her courage at the same time it knocked the wind right out of her sails.

Chapter Ten

Barefooted, her feet propped on a large leather hassock, Cindy nursed a glass of iced tea and whispered words she'd repeated silently at least a dozen times since she'd gotten home from work an hour ago. "I can't believe I did it. One day—one interview, and I'm gainfully employed at a place where people actually sell hats!"

Granted, the hats were nothing she'd be caught dead wearing. For the most part they were dull, tweedy things for the town-and-country set, or Sunday-go-to-meeting hats for the older generation.

They all could have done with a few of her special touches. Her signature touches, as she liked to think of them. Half a dozen blossoms around the crown with a single blossom half-hidden under the brim. Or a mass of delicate mixed flowers swathed in yards of pastel tulle, like a florist's bouquet wrapped in tissue.

Hitch came in, sank into his favorite chair and lifted his feet to share the hassock. We're like an old married couple, she thought, only of course, they weren't. They were strictly temporary.

Like her job.

"You got lucky," he said, and she nodded. She'd walked right out of the interview and onto the floor. Trying out, they'd told her, but she'd found out later that they were desperate for short-term help. Claire from the nearby cosmetics counter filled in whenever a customer showed up in headwear.

"Actually, Marston's got lucky," he amended. He was wearing a shirt she had ironed with her own two hands. The collar was open and the cuffs turned back. He had absolutely gorgeous forearms, tanned under a dusting of crisp, dark hair.

"Thanks. I think so, too."

"How long do you think it'll be before they make you manager? A week? Six weeks?" He was teasing, of course. She hadn't told him just how tenuous her job security was.

"I'd rather be a buyer than a manager. Whoever selects their stock has no imagination at all."

"Why not take in a few of your creations? Show 'em what a real hat looks like. Give yourself a week or so first to get the feel of the place."

He wasn't serious, but the truth was, she had thought of it. "You think that's a hat?" she would say. "Now *this* is a hat!"

"Well." She drained her glass and set it on a coaster. "As to that, there's some good news and some bad news."

"I'm afraid to ask."

"You don't have to worry, you won't be stuck with me. The good news is that if they like me, they'll consider me for part-time and I can pretty well count on at least three days a week once the fall season gets under way." She smiled, a little too brightly. "The bad news is that next week the regular clerk will be back from maternity leave."

"The hell you say." Hitch's feet hit the floor. "Then why'd they advertise it?"

"They didn't. Your secretary knew about it because she's friends with Claire from cosmetics. She thought it might turn into something long-term. And it still might...eventually."

After a while he said, "But no guarantees, huh? Hard to believe that only a few years ago people went to work and stayed on the job until they were handed a gold watch and turned out to pasture."

"I never wanted that, anyway. I told you I intend to start my own business."

"Believe me, there's no security there, either. When you're working for yourself you put in killer hours with no pension waiting on the other end. Whatever happens, it's your responsibility. Remind me to show you the stats on first-year failures."

"You can show me, but that won't stop me from trying."

"I didn't think it would. Go for it then, but don't bite off more than you can chew."

"Sounds like a plan," she said, and they both smiled. Warmly, tiredly, as comfortable together as two people could be when they were both aware of the undercurrents swirling around them.

He had shucked off his moccasins. Now he lifted

his bare feet back onto the hassock, alongside hers.
Together they stared at the two pairs of feet, trying
to ignore the tension that made the room seem suddenly airless. She had never thought of feet as having gender. Now she did. His, long, narrow, high arched, were decidedly masculine.

Hers were much smaller. She wiggled her toes. She was tempted to—

Don't you dare.

"I bought two dresses and a pair of shoes on sale today. They let me have my employee's discount, even though I'm not really entitled yet. Claire said they're embarrassed because the pay is so low, but I'm entitled to a one percent sales commission."

"Won't even offset the deductions."

"It's still more than I've ever earned before. Of course, I won't get paid right away, but tomorrow I'm planning to look at an efficiency apartment Claire told me about."

"No way."

She withdrew her feet and twisted in her chair. "Hitch, we agreed on this, remember? The minute I could afford it I was going to get a place of my own? Well, I can afford it now. I have my savings back, and thanks to you, I have a bank and everything."

"What happens when your replacement shows up and you're back to pounding the pavement?"

"I—I'll just pound it, that's all. I had good luck the first time. Now that I've been through my first job interview, I'm not worried. I can—"

When the telephone rang, Hitch murmured an

apology and reached for it. "Hitchcock," he said quietly, his eyes never leaving her face.

She knew from the way he was listening that something was wrong. His eyes narrowed. The angles of his face actually seemed to grow sharper. By the time he spoke, he was already on his feet. "I'll be there," he said calmly, almost reassuringly. "I can leave within the hour. I'll go directly to the hospital."

The hospital.

Memories, none of them good, swept her back through time. She wanted to ask what had happened, and thought, not Steff. Oh, Lord, not Mac, too! Was it today when they were supposed to fly home?

"I've got to leave," he said as soon as he hung up.

"Is it—someone I know?"

He shook his head. Ramming his feet back into his moccasins, he said, "My father's had a stroke. Apparently, it's not the first one. My mother didn't see fit to call me before, but this one's big. She's falling apart, and my mother never falls apart."

"What can I do?" Cindy said simply.

On the move, he shot off a few suggestions. After the second one she grabbed a notepad and started scribbling. Phone numbers. People to contact. Appointments Sara would need to reschedule.

"Here are the keys to the apartment. I'm going to throw a few things in a bag. Can you hold down the fort for a few days?"

"Should I call Marston's and—"

"Oh, hell no. Don't do that, there's no reason at all for you to sit by the phone. Work. Shop. Do whatever you'd normally do. I'll check in with you as soon as I know something. If you're not here, I'll leave a message.''

A few minutes later she handed him his new glasses—he'd forgotten and left them on the mantel. "You'd better take these. And don't worry about anything here. I'll call Sara and she'll call your partner, and we'll handle whatever comes up.''

His face softened and he gazed down at her for a long moment. "I know you will. And Cindy—"

"It will be all right, I know it will. If your father's anything at all like you, he's strong and tough and resilient."

"He's not at all—" He broke off, a bitter smile touching his mouth, if not his eyes. "Yeah, maybe he is, at that."

And then, his overnight bag in one hand, he kissed her. She knew what was coming and met him halfway. For one long moment they clung together, sharing hopes, sharing fears, sharing strength.

"Call me," she whispered. *I love you. I know you don't want me to, but if love helps, you have all of mine.*

Hitch called from the hospital. He gave her the guarded prognosis and told her he'd stay on a few days if she didn't mind keeping up with his mail and messages. Still unable to believe that the parents he'd thought invincible all these years weren't, he told Cindy his mother needed him.

"He's probably going to be totally helpless," Janet Hitchcock had said over and over, her voice unrecognizable, as if any lessening of her husband's legendary power was inconceivable.

"You don't know that," Hitch told her, trying to sound confident when he felt anything but. It was as if their roles had suddenly been reversed. "We'll start getting the house ready, have his bed moved to the first floor, line up the best nurses and whatever other help you'll need. It's probably too soon for therapists, but I'll check into it."

"You'll stay, won't you? Surely that job of yours can do without you for a few days."

That job of his. The career he'd fought for so bitterly. The company that had been named by the chamber of commerce as one of the ten most successful new firms for the last two years in a row.

"With your father—with your father—"

Oh, hell, she was going to cry. Women like his mother didn't cry, they drove lesser mortals to tears.

But he held her, and she dampened his shirt, then apologized and pulled away. "This isn't like me," she whispered.

"Bend a little, Mother. You weren't born in a courtroom," he said, wanting her to understand—or maybe needing to convince himself—that like everyone else, she possessed hidden strengths that could be exposed like rock strata, by erosion or by cataclysm.

Unfortunately, those same forces could also uncover weaknesses.

"Almost," she said with a broken laugh. "My mother refused to leave until Father's senate hearing was over. He was up for Supreme Court, and you know how partisan those things can be. I was born on the way to the hospital.''

"I never knew that," he said. As a child, he'd had it drilled into him that his family on both sides had comprised the backbone of the nation's legal system for countless generations.

He'd figured it was time someone broke the monopoly.

A nurse came to tell them there was a room available if Judge Hitchcock would like to lie down.

Judge Hitchcock would not, thank you. Judge Hitchcock had standards to maintain. Decorum, and all that, Hitch thought with a mixture of tenderness and impatience.

The doctor came to tell them they would know more after the latest tests had been evaluated, but things looked guardedly optimistic. Hitch talked his mother into relaxing her vaunted standards for once in her life.

"You're not going to do anyone any good if you collapse," he reasoned.

She lifted the famous Hitchcock eyebrow, but for once the effect was lost, due possibly to red-rimmed eyes and a newly haggard look. "Oh, all right, if you insist, but only for an hour. Stand outside the door and see that no one comes in. I won't have anyone seeing me sleeping.''

"Yes, ma'am. No, ma'am,'' he responded, like the dutiful son he'd never been.

Funny, he mused, after a few hours had passed and he was on his third cup of coffee. People projected a certain image, and the world took them at face value.

Cindy, for instance. A kid, he'd thought at first. A spunky, hot-tempered kid. A doormat, a flake, a funny, cheerful creature who had no business being so damned sexy with a faceful of freckles and a sackful of ridiculous dreams.

Two days later, Cindy and her faceful of freckles and her sackful of ridiculous dreams showed up at the hospital. She was wearing what was evidently one of her new dresses. It was yellow, a long, flowery skirt with a soft knit top. She looked beautiful.

She also managed to look both determined and uncertain.

Hitch was in the solarium, so called because of the six large windows, while his mother was in with his father. Pulling rank, she had talked the doctor into releasing him as soon as the next battery of tests were finished, claiming she could afford whatever was needed by way of equipment and staff, and besides, George would respond much faster in familiar territory.

Hitch had a feeling it was his mother who needed to be back on her own turf, where she was in full command. At least she was regaining her cool, as one of the nurses put it.

Hell on wheels was the phrase another one had used.

"I probably shouldn't have come, but Sara and Buck said they could take care of things there, but they're worried about you."

"Buck?" His partner's name was Miller Grove.

"He asked me to call him that. He's real nice, but Hitch, you look awful."

"Thanks," he replied, resisting the urge to sweep her into his arms and hold on for the next dozen or so years.

"It's this place," she told him gravely. "There's so much hurt inside these walls that nobody can really relax. After a while it gets you down. What you need is a—"

"James, who is this person?"

Janet Hitchcock had come into the solarium unnoticed. Although obviously under severe strain, she couldn't possibly have looked more imperious.

"Mother, this is Cynthia Danbury, an old friend of mine dating back to my college days."

Cindy smiled and extended her hand.

The judge extended her backbone another half inch and ignored the overture.

"My mother's tired," Hitch said grimly. "She doesn't mean to be rude, but she hasn't had much sleep lately."

Both women ignored him. "Are you the woman he's been living with?"

"Yes, but not the way you mean it."

"How the devil did you know about—that Cindy was—" Hitch broke off, shaking his head.

"Hitch rescued me from an unpleasant situation, and now he's helping me get started in my business. I have an apartment of my own all ready to move into as soon as the painters are done with it."

Hitch stared at her. "The devil you say."

She smiled sweetly, then turned back to the older woman. "I'm from a real small town, and I've never been away from home before. I didn't realize how much I didn't know until I tackled finding a job and a place to live, but you don't want to hear about me." She turned to Hitch, who was feeling somewhat superfluous at the moment. "How is your daddy? The nurse wouldn't tell me anything."

Hitch started to speak, but his mother cut him off. "He's doing as well as can be expected, thank you for inquiring. I know you must be anxious to leave before the traffic gets too dreadful."

"It's something, all right. I must have driven around the same block half a dozen times before I found a parking place."

Taking both women by the arm, Hitch steered them to an alcove and insisted on seating them. "Mother, sit before you drop. If Father's going home anytime soon you'll need your strength." He turned to Cindy then. "Mind my asking how you got here? And don't tell me you took a cab."

"I bought a car."

"You bought a *what?*"

"James, don't shout," his mother, ever the judge, said.

Hitch said, "Mother, butt out." To Cindy he said, "What do you mean, you bought a car?"

So then she had to explain. To the judge, she said, "I already own a car that my uncle gave me for my eighteenth birthday, but it was old then and it's even older now, and besides, it's back in Mocksville—that's in North Carolina—and it would cost over three hundred dollars to fix. I don't think that's sensible, do you?"

Janet Hitchcock stared at her as if she were something under a microscope.

"Yes, well, I thought so, too, so I bought this

secondhand car that used to belong to an elderly woman who didn't need it anymore. The thing is, I didn't realize how much all the extras cost.''

''I assume you have a valid driver's license?''

''Oh, yes, ma'am. I'm an excellent driver. That's what I did in my last job—actually, it was my own business.''

''You were a chauffeur?''

Encouraged by the way Hitch's poor mama was entering into the conversation, Cindy went on to describe her Monday thing. Told her about some of the more amusing incidents that had occurred over the years, and how she'd had to keep it secret, which wasn't easy in a town the size of Mocksville, because Aunt S. had her dignity, after all.

''Sometimes I think dignity is a little overrated, don't you? I mean, when it keeps you from seeing what's important and what's not, what good is it?''

His mother was beginning to look slightly dazed. With more than a hint of desperation, Hitch said, ''Look, why don't I bring us something from the cafeteria?''

''Oh, sit down, James. I don't eat in public waiting rooms, and Miss—Miss—''

''Cindy,'' Cindy supplied helpfully.

''Cindy can wait until we get your father home. I'm sure Mrs. Kueber will have a meal prepared—she knows we'll be there for dinner.''

And they were. All four of them, plus a nurse and the Hitchcocks' driver, a man with the unlikely name of Bloodstock.

Bloodstock and the nurse dined in the kitchen.

The judge had a tray served in her husband's room. Hitch and Cindy sat at either end of a table that was fully ten feet long, in a room so formal Cindy half expected to be hustled out at any moment.

As if starved, they both tackled the shallow bowls of pale bouillon. There was a slice of lemon floating on the surface. Cindy was tempted to devour that, too, but since Hitch didn't, she didn't, either.

The edge taken off their appetites, just barely, he said, "Now, would you mind telling me what the devil you're doing here?"

The housekeeper-cook entered quietly and set two plates before them. Cindy stared down at the tiny portion of beef, oozing red juice. There was one sprig of something green on the edge of the translucent china plate, and a spoonful of rice with flecks of something gray in it. On a smaller plate there was a roll so hard it could have doubled as a cannonball, and one tiny rosebud of butter.

Oh, for a double cheeseburger with bacon and fries.

"Well, I knew all along my job was short-term, only they sort of led me to believe I could stay on part-time. But the woman I was replacing came back, and there's not enough business for one clerk, much less two. They would've let me work out the rest of the week, but I said no thank you." She poked at the rice and tasted a forkful. "Try this, it's pretty good."

"Cindy, I'm waiting. I warn you, I'm on an extremely short fuse."

"I thought you might be, which is why I came. I dreamed you were calling me, and after all you did for me when I needed a friend, it was the least I could do in return.''

He shook his head in reluctant admiration. Either she was one hell of an actress, or the astigmatism he'd just had corrected had messed up more than his eyesight. ''All right, cut the act. You might play the small-town ingenue, but we both know you're a lot smarter than most people give you credit for being.''

He waited for a denial—for any response at all—and when she merely nodded and cut into her morsel of beef, he went on. ''Cindy, you met my mother. You see the setup here. It's hardly what anyone could call user-friendly. I'm amazed she's let you stay even this long.''

''Mmm, beef's good, too.' Cindy swallowed. ''She didn't let me stay, Hitch, she wants me here. I know—she didn't say so, but I can tell. I'm not sure why yet—I'll probably figure it out sooner or later, but this place needs something, and she knows it, and as an outsider, I just might be able to put my finger on it. Your mother's stressed out. I don't know about your father, I hardly even saw him, but your mother's smart enough to know that if she doesn't ease up, she's going to crack wide open, only she doesn't know how to ease up. In some ways, she reminds me of Aunt S.''

He could only shake his head in reluctant admiration. ''You're something else, you know that?''

''Yes, well—we all are, aren't we? Something else, I mean. Only we're all a lot more alike underneath than some of us care to admit. We all hurt, only some of us don't know how to handle it. We all strive, only some of us strive harder than others.

We're all mortal, but some of us would rather not think about it. At least,'' she added, somewhat embarrassed, ''that's what I think.''

The whole house moved as if on tiptoe. Staff included, nobody spoke above a quiet murmur. Hitch thought about what Cindy had said, about hurting and striving and being afraid to face mortality.

Was that his mother's problem? Having reigned supreme for so long, was she so afraid to admit there were things over which she had no control that she would turn to a stranger rather than admit a weakness to someone she knew?

Yeah, now that it had been pointed out to him, he could see how it might be true. All these years they'd reacted to one another without taking time to think. His parents, even a few of his elder cousins, had reacted to his going to engineering school as rank heresy. He, in turn, had interpreted their reaction as high-handed arrogance.

It took someone like Cindy, with her combination of naivete and wisdom, to see through all the crap, all the defensive posturing.

Lying awake that night in his old room, he thought about the woman in the room just down the hall. Was she asleep? What did she think—what did she *really* think—of his folks? It had been so long since he'd considered them as individuals. As real people with dreams and goals and fears. He was beginning to believe he should have had his eyes examined a long time ago.

Or maybe his head.

Ah, Cindy, Cindy, what am I going to do about you?

She didn't fit into his life any more than she fit into his parents' lives, yet here she was. And somehow, he could no longer imagine life without her.

Chapter Eleven

"Now, this one I call Mother-of-Pearl," Cindy said as she carefully lifted another hat from the bag and settled it on her head.

"No, she doesn't," Hitch said dryly. "She calls it Pearl's Mama."

Janet Hitchcock's tired gray eyes moved from one to the other. "Indeed..."

It occurred to Hitch that his mother's face had lost some of the waxy pallor he'd observed earlier. He didn't know if she wore makeup or not. If so, it wasn't obvious. He glanced across the still figure lying on the hospital bed, caught Cindy's anxious eyes and gave her an imperceptible thumbs-up.

She hadn't wanted to do it. He'd talked her into it.

"A fashion show," she'd exclaimed. "Hitch, that's just plain crazy! I can't do that, not in this house. Not with your parents. Especially at a time like this, with your father sick. It would be—it would be inappropriate.''

Inappropriate. It was one of his mother's favorite words. God knows, most of his life had been deemed inappropriate.

Oddly enough, he no longer felt that way. ''Humor me. It's just what this old mausoleum needs, and Mother could do with a distraction. Got anything in that bag of yours that goes with a black robe?''

''Be serious,'' Cindy chided.

''I am serious.'' He wasn't even sure himself why he'd suggested it, but watching her put on one absurd hat after another and strike a pose in his father's gloomy sickroom, he knew he'd been right. He didn't know whether or not his father was even aware of what was going on, but he had to believe that inside that still form there existed the same razor-sharp brain, the same pride in his wife's accomplishments, the same impatience with his only son, that had made growing up here such hell.

Hitch prayed to God it was all still there, but at any rate, they could do with a distraction. For perhaps the first time in their lives, his parents were powerless. That would be stressful enough for an ordinary mortal, but for someone accustomed to unquestioned, unilateral authority, it had to be terrifying.

His mother was visibly crumbling. Yesterday at the hospital he'd noticed the fine tremor in her hands. Today, she hadn't even bothered to put her hair up. Never, to his knowledge, had Janet Hale Hitchcock emerged from her bedroom less than fully dressed, fully groomed—girded to right the wrongs of the world.

Now, confronted with a redheaded stranger wearing baggy jeans and pink sneakers, with a full-blown garden fantasy on her head, she was totally nonplussed. To Hitch's way of thinking, it was a hell of a lot better than being fearful, tearful or depressed.

"It's very...nice," the judge murmured.

Cindy turned to the still, silent figure on the hospital bed, which had been hastily set up in the study. Hitch had made all arrangements for that and for the team of round-the-clock nurses before the hospital would release the patient. "Mr. Hitchcock, this one is supposed to appeal to a man. What do you think? Wink if you like it, frown if you don't."

The patient did neither, of course. Yet it seemed to Hitch that his father's eyes twinkled in a face that was both older and oddly younger than he remembered. Gone were the deep lines that had dominated those stern features for as long as he could recall.

"I didn't bring all my hats," Cindy explained. She looked as out of place as a rainbow in a coal mine in the dark, walnut-paneled room, with its heavy furniture and its walls lined with leather-bound tomes. "I have eleven complete designs and materials for a few more, but you have to understand, they're only working models. Sometimes I rob Peter to pay Paul, so to speak."

"Yes, of course," the judge murmured politely. She looked somewhat dazed. She'd had that same look more than once lately.

Way to go, sweetheart, Hitch cheered silently.

Never in a million years would he have invited her here. Hell, he wouldn't do that to his worst enemy, if he had an enemy.

It had been Cindy's own decision to come. She claimed to have heard him calling her in her dreams. And he had to admit he'd never been so glad to see anyone in his entire life than when he'd looked up to see a redheaded, freckle-faced vision standing uncertainly in the doorway of the solarium. He'd felt warm all over, with the kind of warmth that kindled deep inside him and spilled over like melted candle wax.

Over that abysmal dinner they'd shared the night before, she'd told him that she could get a room somewhere and drive back tomorrow if he didn't need her. Or she could look for a job and a place to stay right here. "There's no law that says I have to stay in Richmond," she'd explained earnestly. "That's the nice thing about being independent. I can go where I want to go, do what I want to do, and nobody cares."

I care, he'd thought, but hadn't dared say it. The time wasn't right, and besides, he had no reason to think she wanted to hear it.

"Cindy, do you think you might do something with all the flowers that have arrived?" Janet asked once the hat show was over. "Perhaps you could bring in a few blossoms from each arrangement. It won't do to show partiality."

Huge arrangements had been arriving all morning, most, to Hitch's way of thinking, designed to impress rather than to cheer. "I'd love to. Something bright is just what this room needs."

"Perhaps you could leave a few of your...bonnets lying around," the judge remarked, which was the closest thing to a joke Hitch had ever heard from her. He nearly fell off his chair.

The rest of the week passed in an exhausting procession of hope, disappointment, adaptations and revelations. At Judge Hitchcock's request, the doctor paid a house call and said it was too soon to expect any change, but things looked promising.

Hitch set up a field office in his bedroom and made one quick trip in the middle of the week to Richmond to deal with a minor crisis. Miller Grove—or Buck, as Cindy called him—was great with ideas, but considerably less great when it came to dealing with clients.

Cindy was a godsend. If asked a week earlier, Hitch would have said she would never in a million years fit into his parents' household. But it was Cindy who took over writing thank-you notes after seeing the ones written by the judge's personal assistant.

It was Cindy who relieved the nurses, reading the daily newspapers and an old C. S. Forrester WWII novel aloud. She even took to working on her hats there, pausing now and then to ask the patient's advice.

"This doesn't look right to me. What d'you think, too much? I could take off these flowers here, or maybe add more to the other side. Hmm."

And then she'd nod her head, just as if she'd received a response.

It was Cindy who called his mother by her given

name. It blew Hitch away. Flat out blew him away the first time he heard her saying, "Janet, you forgot to eat breakfast this morning. Annie and I made muffins."

Annie. She was on a first-name basis with the staff, too. So far as Hitch knew, no one had ever called the woman who presided over the kitchen like a five-star general anything other than Mrs. Kueber.

That night, Hitch took advantage of a rare moment alone with Cindy to thank her for all she'd done. They'd met outside the study, Hitch on his way up to his room to deal with the latest batch of faxes and e-files, Cindy on some errand of her own.

"I don't know how to thank you. You've made—"

She laid a finger over his lips. That was her first mistake. Touching him. He captured the finger, kissed it and then curled her hand into his. "I'm serious. It's like breaching the Great Wall of China or the Berlin Wall. You've got 'em eating out of your hand—my mother, even my father. I'm almost sure I saw him trying to smile when you were telling him about the way I nearly ran you down."

By then she was practically in his arms, messing up his mind with the warm, flowery scent of her hair. "Thanks for giving away my secrets, by the way," he growled softly.

She smiled—it was actually more of a grin, but it did it to him all over again. That melted-candle-wax feeling. So he kissed her, and might even have carried her upstairs to his bedroom for another kiss—and more—if the sound of his mother's brisk footsteps hadn't broken the spell.

Breathless, they stared at each other. "I know now why you're called Cindy," he murmured.

"I told you that," she said, now standing a safe three feet away.

Ignoring her comment, he said, "It's short for Incendiary." Raising his voice, he said, "Mother, do you mind if I tie up your fax line for a few minutes?"

With a regal nod, Janet Hitchcock gave permission. Hitch thought, *Saved by the bell.* If his mother had bothered to look at him she'd have thrown the book at him, or at least given him a lecture on moral turpitude.

But then, she might not even recognize his condition...although she and his father must have thawed out at least once in the early years of their marriage, else he wouldn't be here.

On Monday of the second week, Janet Hitchcock suggested that it was time for her son to return to Richmond. "It's not as if there's anything you can do here. George's recovery will be a slow process, and I'm sure you have your own life to lead."

It was a mark of how much he'd relaxed his guard that the words cut to the quick. "Yeah, you're right. We might as well take off. You can always call if there's any change."

The judge lifted one eyebrow. Both brows would have meant "You're out of line, sir."

A single elevated brow meant "You are dangerously close to being held in contempt of court."

He waited to hear the charges. He'd already heard the sentence. "You want to give me a clue?"

"Cindy can stay on. George seems to enjoy having her around."

For a long moment Hitch couldn't think of a thing to say. He told himself it had been a stressful time for all—for his mother more than anyone—besides which, she'd never been known for her tact.

But it was a little too much like being ten years old and being told that his father had more important things to do than watch him play football. Or having Bloodstock take him to see a carefully selected film for his birthday because the birthday party he'd asked for did not fit into their schedule.

"I'll leave that up to Cindy."

"She'll stay if I tell her to stay."

"If you ask her, you mean."

The eyebrow thing again.

"All right, Mother, ask her. It's your house."

She nodded, turned and walked away, and Hitch told himself to cut his losses and get the hell out of there before he blew up and said something unforgivable. For a little while he'd felt almost like a member of the family.

But then, it wasn't the first time he'd been deluded.

What the hell—he didn't need them any more than they needed him. As for Cindy, she was free to make her own choices. That was what independence was all about, wasn't it? And that was what she wanted above all. To call her own shots.

Although to be fair, someone should warn her that independence wasn't a priority under the Hitchcock regime. Or even a possibility. But then, Cindy had grown up under pretty much the same type of system. Maybe she felt safer that way.

It took him less than five minutes to pack his overnight bag, somewhat longer to shut down and pack up his portable office. Not until he'd loaded everything into his car did he go in search of Cindy.

He found her in the pantry, lifting flowers from a gargantuan arrangement more suitable for the winner of a horse race, and placing them loosely in a dented pewter pitcher. "Annie said she'll look for a few bright, inexpensive vases next time she goes shopping."

"I came to say goodbye."

Flowers. He would always picture her surrounded by flowers, smelling of flowers, grimy, green-stained fingers and all.

She lifted a stricken face to his. "You're leaving?"

"Mother says you're welcome to stay, the choice is yours." He made no effort to sway her judgment one way or the other, but it was tough. What he wanted to say was, "Let's get the hell out of here before they take over your life the way they tried to take over mine. If anyone's going to take over your life, dammit, it's going to be me!"

"But your father—"

"Doesn't need me."

"Of course he does." She wiped her hands down the sides of her shirt and then planted them on her hips. "Just because he can't say so in words right now, that doesn't mean he doesn't know you're here, and—and he wants you here. I know. I can tell by the way his eyes follow you when you're in the room, like he's trying to tell you something, only he can't, and—and—"

Hitch expelled a harsh sigh. "Cindy, you're a dreamer. You've admitted it yourself. Me, I deal in reality."

"No, you don't. You're a dreamer, too. Dreams are real, else there wouldn't be a name for them. We all know what dreams are, only some of us are afraid to believe in them."

"Look, I can't fight this." He shrugged. "Believe what you want to believe, only don't forget that a big part of that dream of yours is to be free to live your own life. Don't get sucked into another Send Cindy situation, okay?"

He hadn't kissed her. All the rest of the day, while she arranged bright, light bouquets and took them to Mr. George—she thought of him that way, even called him that—she thought about Hitch, and why he didn't seem to get along with either of his parents, and what a waste it was.

And she wondered why he hadn't kissed her. It wasn't as if they'd chosen up sides and she'd picked them over him. Right now they needed her. They were a part of him, whether or not he wanted to acknowledge it. And if there was any way she could bring them together, she had to try.

She took her supper tray in Mr. George's room so that the night nurse could take off her shoes and relax while she ate and watched *Wheel of Fortune*. Janet, exhausted, was napping.

"Well, I guess you know he's gone," she said to

Hitch's father as she tasted her soup. Annie was getting better about seasoning, but she wasn't there yet. Still, nobody had complained.

"You ought to taste this, it's really pretty good. Maybe by the time you're ready to tackle real food again, I'll have taught Annie how to make ham bone soup. Now there's a meal fit for a king."

There was no response, of course, but she was pretty sure Mr. George's expression lifted just a bit. Something about his eyes. They were gray, shaped exactly like Hitch's, only not as dark. Both his parents had gray eyes.

"Yes, well...as I was saying, Hitch left early this afternoon. I think he believes you don't want him here. I told him you did—that just because you couldn't ask him to stay, that didn't mean you didn't want him here, but you know how he is. Stubborn as a mule. He gets this notion in his head, and nothing will shake it loose."

She shoved her tray aside, leaned back in the massive leather chair and shook her head. "He thinks you and Janet don't love him. Not that he would ever say so, but you can tell. I don't know where on earth he could have gotten that idea, because he's the kind of son any parent would be proud to have. He's sort of a—well, I guess you might say he's a cross between an artist and an engineer. He's intelligent, but at the same time he's intuitive. He's practical and yet he's creative. He also happens to be the kindest, dearest, most generous man in the world, and if he wasn't so dead set against marriage, I'd marry him in a minute."

Under cover of her thick lashes, Cindy studied the

man on the bed. She hadn't imagined it. Something in his face had moved. There was a look in his eyes that told her he was struggling to express himself.

Yes! Please God, because until Hitch knows his parents love him, he won't believe anyone else can. We've got our work cut out for us here, so let's get on with it.

Hitch waited as long as he could before calling. The housekeeper answered on the kitchen extension. "Mrs. Kueber, is Miss Danbury available?"

"I'm sure she is, sir. She just left to take your mother her cocoa and stress vitamins. We're all taking them now, and I do believe they're helping. Things, if you don't mind my saying so, are considerably more comfortable around here just lately."

Hitch could have told her it was vitamin Cindy that was making the difference, but he didn't. "I'll hold," he said.

He heard her even before she picked up the phone. She was running. No one ever, to his knowledge, ran in his parents' house. It was unseemly.

"Hitch?"

She sounded breathless. He knew that sound. He missed it, God how he missed it! "Is everything going okay?"

"Except that we miss you. Your father most of all, I think, but your mother showed me your baby pictures today. She got all soft and sort of weepy, but that's only natural. Everyone's under a strain."

He didn't know whether to laugh or swear. His *baby* pictures? Hell, he hadn't even known she'd ever had one taken, much less kept the thing. "I just thought I'd better check to be sure you were doing okay.'' He'd seen her only yesterday. It seemed more like a year.

"Could you maybe come back this weekend? I know your work is piling up, but Buck doesn't mind doing double duty as long as he has Sara to talk to people. Did you know they're in love? With each other, I mean?''

Hitch's jaw fell. As long as he'd known them— as invaluable as they were to the success of the business—he hadn't given more than a passing thought to their private lives.

"Well, actually,'' she continued, "I'm not sure they know it themselves yet, but they will. You can always tell when the steam builds up, can't you? The kettle starts to rock and the lid starts to rattle.''

Rock and rattle, he thought a few minutes later as he gently replaced the phone in its cradle. Was that what was happening to him? He could vouch for the buildup of steam, but he'd like to believe he hadn't yet started to rattle.

He hadn't given her an answer about the weekend because the answer he would have given wasn't the one she wanted to hear. Which was the reason he wasn't prepared when he unlocked his door and was surrounded by the smell of pot roast and flowers.

"Hello?'' he called out cautiously.

The bathroom door opened in a cloud of steam. A towel-clad, turbanned figure leaned out. "Hitch! Oh, heck, I wanted to be all dressed and everything when you got home.''

Candle wax. That was the only way to describe

it, the warm, melting feeling that spilled over him. It was followed almost immediately by a feeling that was hotter and harder than any melted candle. "When did you get here?"

Stupid question. *Why* was she here? Had she chosen him over his parents, after all? Was she here because she had nowhere else to go?

"I hope you don't mind. We need to talk, and I thought we could talk better on a full stomach."

It wasn't his stomach he was concerned about at the moment. And conversation could wait, too. "Yeah, sure. Anything I can do to help?" He dropped his briefcase and tried not to stare at the line of demarcation showing just above the bath towel. The freckles didn't extend down as far as the swell of her breasts.

He almost wished they did; he'd have enjoyed counting them.

"Just give me a minute to get dressed," she said, and ducked back into the bathroom.

Three minutes later she emerged again, dressed in his bathrobe, her hair wet and several shades darker. "Want to eat first and then talk?"

"I'd rather make love, then eat, then talk."

Her eyes goggled. There was no other word for it. "Make *what?*"

"What's the matter, didn't you dry your ears?"

She came into the room, shifted her hat bag off the chair and sat down, primly tucking the flaps of his bathrobe over her knees. "What's got into you? You've never said anything like that before, at least not to me."

"No? Then it's about time I did, isn't it?"

She waited, her brow furrowed as she studied him in the fading light falling through the window. September. The days were getting shorter.

His mind shifted briefly to philosophical mode, but the demands of his body quickly overrode it. "I wasn't sure I'd ever see you again," he said, going cold at hearing the thought voiced aloud. It had been wearing on him ever since he'd driven away—that he might have thrown away something of inestimable value.

That she might go through life never knowing that there was a man who loved her more than he'd ever dreamed possible.

Hell, she'd taught him the meaning of the word.

"Come here," he said gruffly, holding out one hand, loosening his tie with the other. "Please?"

She flew to his arms, a look on her face that was almost like...relief? Could she possibly have had doubts?

He'd had plenty of his own, but then, that was different. He'd been conditioned early on not to look for love. Neither of his parents knew the meaning of the word, and nothing that had happened since had taught him otherwise. Love—the romantic kind—was an illusion. A fairy tale that as a rational adult he refused to buy into.

Feeling the warm, fragrant woman burrowing into his arms, her wet hair plastered against his cheek, he stopped thinking at all. He had better things to do at the moment.

"I love you," he whispered a long time later.

"Don't ever stop," she said simply. "I couldn't bear it."

His arms tightened around her. A red sunrise cast a warm glow across the room. "What, a lifetime guarantee? You've got it."

Warm kisses followed. Murmured words. They were both starved for breakfast, but hungrier still for each other.

Time passed in a sweet, warm haze. After a while Hitch murmured drowsily, "What's it going to be, love? Another home wedding? Would you like to go back to Mocksville?"

Cindy considered it for a full minute, then shook her head. "How about in your father's study, so he can be there? Can't judges perform weddings?"

Hitch closed his eyes and laughed softly. "You're a miracle worker, sweetheart, but don't push your luck."

"It's not luck, it's love. We can push all we want, because love stretches."

"Stretches, hmm? Sounds interesting."

"It stretches to cover parents and grandparents, and children—and stepaunts and stepcousins, and—and their spouses, and—"

He laid a finger across her lips. "They're all invited—Aunt S. as long as she promises not to take over. Mac and Steff—they're back by the way—and Maura, if New York can spare her. But for now, what do you say we scale it back to two people and one big easy chair?"

"And maybe a kitchen?"

"Yeah," he growled softly. "Maybe a kitchen."

*   *   *   *   *

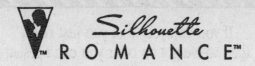

Silhouette

ROMANCE™

COMING NEXT MONTH

#1456 FALLING FOR GRACE—Stella Bagwell
An Older Man

The moment Jack Barrett saw his neighbor, he wanted to know everything about her. Soon he learned beautiful Grace Holliday was pregnant and alone…and too young for him. He also found out she needed protection—from *his* jaded heart….

#1457 THE BORROWED GROOM—Judy Christenberry
The Circle K Sisters

One thing held Melissa Kennedy from her dream of running a foster home—she was single. Luckily, her sexy ranch foreman, Rob Hanson, was willing to be her counterfeit fiancé, but could Melissa keep her borrowed groom…forever?

#1458 DENIM & DIAMOND—Moyra Tarling

Kyle Masters was shocked when old friend Piper Diamond asked him to marry her. He wasn't looking for a wife, yet how could he refuse when without him, she could lose custody of her unborn child? It also didn't hurt that she was a stunning beauty….

#1459 THE MONARCH'S SON—Valerie Parv
The Carramer Crown

One minute she'd washed ashore at the feet of a prince, the next, commoner Allie Carter found herself "companion" to Lorne de Marigny's son…and falling for the brooding monarch. He claimed his heart was off-limits, yet his kisses suggested something else!

#1460 JODIE'S MAIL-ORDER MAN—Julianna Morris
Bridal Fever!

Jodie Richards was sick of seeking Mr. Right, so she decided to marry her trustworthy pen pal. But when she went to meet him, she found his brother, Donovan Masters, in his place. And with one kiss, her plan for a passionless union was in danger….

#1461 LASSOED!—Martha Shields

Pose as a model for a cologne ad? That was the *last* job champion bull-rider Tucker Reeves wanted. That is, until a bull knocked him out…and Tucker woke up to lovely photographer Cassie Burch. Could she lasso this cowboy's hardened heart for good?

CMN0600

SILHOUETTE'S 20TH ANNIVERSARY CONTEST
OFFICIAL RULES
NO PURCHASE NECESSARY TO ENTER

1. To enter, follow directions published in the offer to which you are responding. Contest begins 1/1/00 and ends on 8/24/00 (the "Promotion Period"). Method of entry may vary. Mailed entries must be postmarked by 8/24/00, and received by 8/31/00.

2. During the Promotion Period, the Contest may be presented via the Internet. Entry via the Internet may be restricted to residents of certain geographic areas that are disclosed on the Web site. To enter via the Internet, if you are a resident of a geographic area in which Internet entry is permissible, follow the directions displayed on-line, including typing your essay of 100 words or fewer telling us "Where In The World Your Love Will Come Alive." On-line entries must be received by 11:59 p.m. Eastern Standard time on 8/24/00. Limit one e-mail entry per person, household and e-mail address per day, per presentation. If you are a resident of a geographic area in which entry via the Internet is permissible, you may, in lieu of submitting an entry on-line, enter by mail, by hand-printing your name, address, telephone number and contest number/name on an 8"x 11" plain piece of paper and telling us in 100 words or fewer "Where In The World Your Love Will Come Alive," and mailing via first-class mail to: Silhouette 20ᵗʰ Anniversary Contest, (in the U.S.) P.O. Box 9069, Buffalo, NY 14269-9069; (In Canada) P.O. Box 637, Fort Erie, Ontario, Canada L2A 5X3. Limit one 8"x 11" mailed entry per person, household and e-mail address per day. On-line and/or 8"x 11" mailed entries received from persons residing in geographic areas in which Internet entry is not permissible will be disqualified. No liability is assumed for lost, late, incomplete, inaccurate, nondelivered or misdirected mail, or misdirected e-mail, for technical, hardware or software failures of any kind, lost or unavailable network connection, or failed, incomplete, garbled or delayed computer transmission or any human error which may occur in the receipt or processing of the entries in the contest.

3. Essays will be judged by a panel of members of the Silhouette editorial and marketing staff based on the following criteria:

   Sincerity (believability, credibility)—50%

   Originality (freshness, creativity)—30%

   Aptness (appropriateness to contest ideas)—20%

   Purchase or acceptance of a product offer does not improve your chances of winning. In the event of a tie, duplicate prizes will be awarded.

4. All entries become the property of Harlequin Enterprises Ltd., and will not be returned. Winner will be determined no later than 10/31/00 and will be notified by mail. Grand Prize winner will be required to sign and return Affidavit of Eligibility within 15 days of receipt of notification. Noncompliance within the time period may result in disqualification and an alternative winner may be selected. All municipal, provincial, federal, state and local laws and regulations apply. Contest open only to residents of the U.S. and Canada who are 18 years of age or older, and is void wherever prohibited by law. Internet entry is restricted solely to residents of those geographical areas in which Internet entry is permissible. Employees of Torstar Corp., their affiliates, agents and members of their immediate families are not eligible. Taxes on the prizes are the sole responsibility of winners. Entry and acceptance of any prize offered constitutes permission to use winner's name, photograph or other likeness for the purposes of advertising, trade and promotion on behalf of Torstar Corp. without further compensation to the winner, unless prohibited by law. Torstar Corp and D.L. Blair, Inc., their parents, affiliates and subsidiaries, are not responsible for errors in printing or electronic presentation of contest or entries. In the event of printing or other errors which may result in unintended prize values or duplication of prizes, all affected contest materials or entries shall be null and void. If for any reason the Internet portion of the contest is not capable of running as planned, including infection by computer virus, bugs, tampering, unauthorized intervention, fraud, technical failures, or any other causes beyond the control of Torstar Corp. which corrupt or affect the administration, secrecy, fairness, integrity or proper conduct of the contest, Torstar Corp. reserves the right, at its sole discretion, to disqualify any individual who tampers with the entry process and to cancel, terminate, modify or suspend the contest or the Internet portion thereof. In the event of a dispute regarding an on-line entry, the entry will be deemed submitted by the authorized holder of the e-mail account submitted at the time of entry. Authorized account holder is defined as the natural person who is assigned to an e-mail address by an Internet access provider, on-line service provider or other organization that is responsible for arranging e-mail address for the domain associated with the submitted e-mail address.

5. Prizes: Grand Prize—a $10,000 vacation to anywhere in the world. Travelers (at least one must be 18 years of age or older) or parent or guardian if one traveler is a minor, must sign and return a Release of Liability prior to departure. Travel must be completed by December 31, 2001, and is subject to space and accommodations availability. Two hundred (200) Second Prizes—a two-book limited edition autographed collector set from one of the Silhouette Anniversary authors: Nora Roberts, Diana Palmer, Linda Howard or Annette Broadrick (value $10.00 each set). All prizes are valued in U.S. dollars.

6. For a list of winners (available after 10/31/00), send a self-addressed, stamped envelope to: Harlequin Silhouette 20ᵗʰ Anniversary Winners, P.O. Box 4200, Blair, NE 68009-4200.

Contest sponsored by Torstar Corp., P.O. Box 9042, Buffalo, NY 14269-9042.

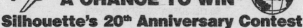

ENTER FOR
A CHANCE TO WIN*

Silhouette's 20th Anniversary Contest

Tell Us Where in the World
You Would Like *Your* Love To Come Alive...
And We'll Send the Lucky Winner There!

Silhouette wants to take you wherever
your happy ending can come true.

Here's how to enter: Tell us, in 100 words or less,
where you want to go to make your love come alive!

In addition to the grand prize, there will be 200
runner-up prizes, collector's-edition book sets
autographed by one of the Silhouette anniversary
authors: **Nora Roberts, Diana Palmer,
Linda Howard** or **Annette Broadrick**.

DON'T MISS YOUR CHANCE TO WIN!
ENTER NOW! No Purchase Necessary

Where love comes alive™

Visit Silhouette at www.eHarlequin.com to enter, starting this summer.

Name: _____

Address: _____

City: _____ State/Province: _____

Zip/Postal Code: _____

Mail to Harlequin Books: **In the U.S.**: P.O. Box 9069, Buffalo, NY
14269-9069; **In Canada**: P.O. Box 637, Fort Erie, Ontario, L4A 5X3

*No purchase necessary—for contest details send a self-addressed stamped envelope to:
Silhouette's 20th Anniversary Contest, P.O. Box 9069, Buffalo, NY, 14269-9069 (include
contest name on self-addressed envelope). Residents of Washington and Vermont may
omit postage. Open to Cdn. (excluding Quebec) and U.S. residents who are 18 or over.
Void where prohibited. Contest ends August 31, 2000.   PS20CON_R2